My dear Rose,

Our visit to the planet of the Firebird was frightening. Fox and I now know that the Snake will do anything to achieve his goal. He won't even hesitate to set an entire planet on fire to stir up jealousy and hatred in the inhabitants.

I'm still having a hard time understanding the grown-ups' idea of power. Power seems to act like a poison, corrupting the hearts of those who possess it. Nevertheless, it seems that every city needs to have a ruler. But what is the ruler's true role? Shouldn't rulers protect their people rather than order them around?

I hope that the next star system we visit will restore my faith in grown-ups. They're such very strange people!

The Little Prince

First American edition published in 2012 by Graphic Universe™.

Le Petit Prince™

based on the masterpiece by Antoine de Saint-Exupéry

© 2012 LPPM
An animated series based on the novel *Le Petit Prince* by Antoine de Saint-Exupéry
Developed for television by Matthieu Delaporte, Alexandre de la Patellière, and Bertrand Gatignol
Directed by Pierre-Alain Chartier

© 2012 ÉDITIONS GLÉNAT
Copyright © 2012 by Lerner Publishing Group, Inc., for the current edition

Graphic Universe™
A division of Lerner Publishing Group, Inc.
241 First Avenue North
Minneapolis, MN 55401 U.S.A.

Website address: www.lernerbooks.com

Library of Congress Cataloging-in-Publication Data

Dorison, Guillaume.
 [Planète de la musique. English]
 The planet of music / by Clélia Constantine ; adapted by Guillaume Dorison ; based on the masterpiece by Antoine de Saint-Exupéry ; illustrated by Élyum Studio, Lucy Mazel, and Jérôme Benoit ; translation, Anne Collins Smith and Owen Smith. — 1st American ed.
  p. cm. — (The little prince ; #03)
  ISBN 978-0-7613-8753-4 (lib. bdg. : alk. paper)
 1. Graphic novels. I. Smith, Anne Collins. II. Smith, Owen. III. Constantine, Clélia. IV. Saint-Exupéry, Antoine de, 1900-1944. Petit Prince. V. Élyum Studio. VI. Petit Prince (Television program) VII. Title.
PZ7.7.D67Ph 2012
741.5'944—dc23   2011051352

Manufactured in the United States of America
1 — DP — 7/15/12

THE NEW ADVENTURES
BASED ON THE MASTERPIECE BY ANTOINE DE SAINT-EXUPÉRY

The Little Prince

THE PLANET OF MUSIC

Based on the animated series and an original story by Clélia Constantine

Design: Élyum Studio
Adaptation: Guillaume Dorison
Artistic Direction: Didier Poli
Art: Lucy Mazel
Backgrounds: Jérôme Benoit
Coloring: Paul Drouin
Editing: Paul Drouin
Editorial Consultant: Didier Convard

Translation: Anne and Owen Smith

Graphic Universe™ • Minneapolis • New York

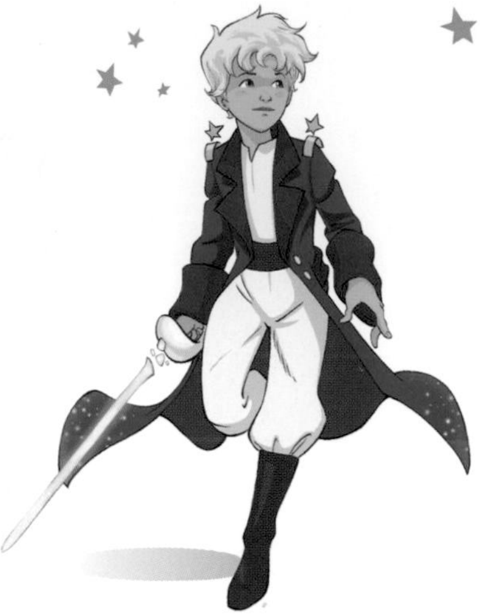

THE LITTLE PRINCE

The Little Prince has extraordinary gifts. His sense of wonder allows him to discover what no one else can see. The Little Prince can communicate with all the beings in the universe, even the animals and plants. His powers grow over the course of his adventures.

The Prince's uniform:
When he wears the uniform of a prince, he is more agile and quick. When faced with difficult situations, the Little Prince also carries a sword that lets him sketch and bring to life anything from his imagination.

His sketchbook:
When he is not in his Prince's clothing, the Little Prince carries a sketchbook. When he blows on the pages, they take wing and form objects that he'll find very useful. Like his sword, it's powered by stardust collected on his travels.

FOX

A grouch, a trickster, and, so he says, interested only in his next meal, Fox is in reality the Little Prince's best friend. As such, he is always there to give him help, but also just as much to help him to grow and to learn about the world.

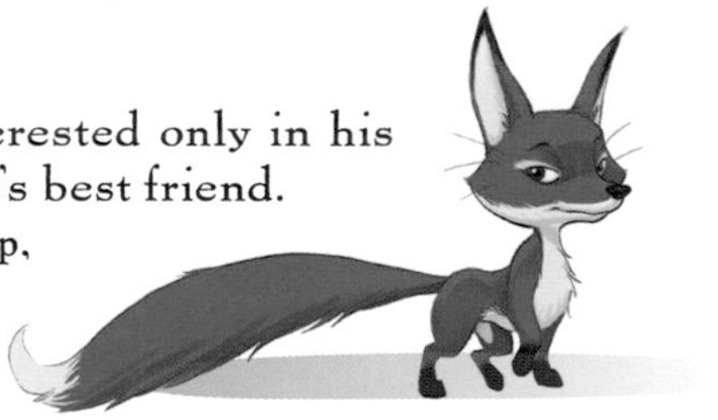

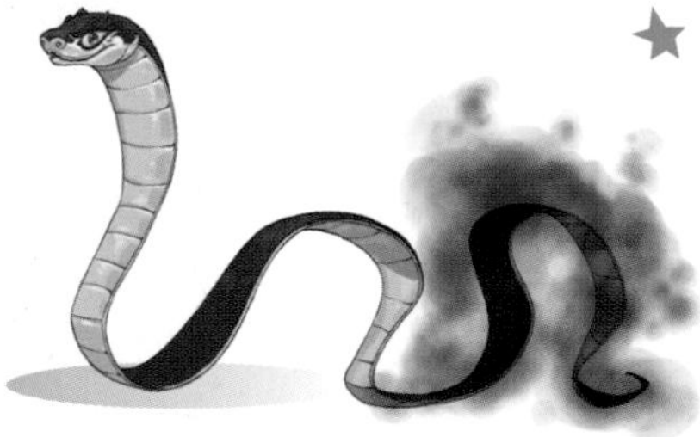

THE SNAKE

Even though the Little Prince still does not know exactly why, there can be no doubt that the Snake has set his mind to plunging the entire universe into darkness! And to accomplish his goal, this malicious being is ready to use any form of deception. However, the Snake never takes action himself. He prefers to bring out the wickedness in those beings he has chosen to bite, tempting them to put their own worlds in danger.

THE GLOOMIES

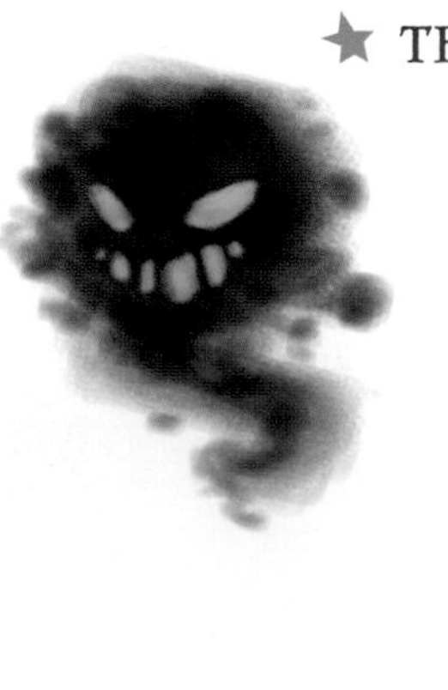

When people who have been "bitten" by the Snake have completely destroyed their own planets, they become Gloomies, slaves to their Snake master. The Gloomies act as a group and carry out the Snake's most vile orders so as to get the better of the Little Prince!

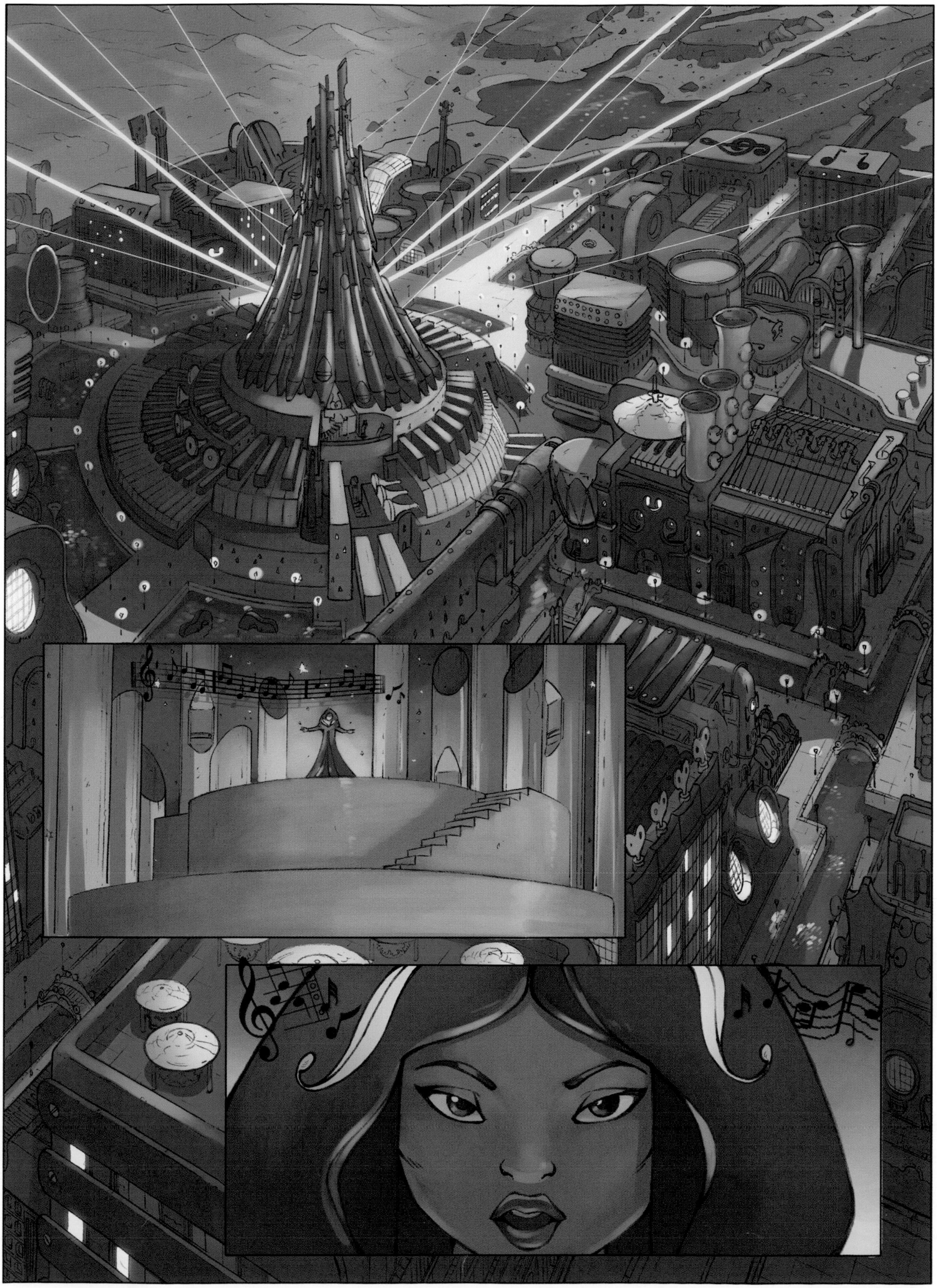

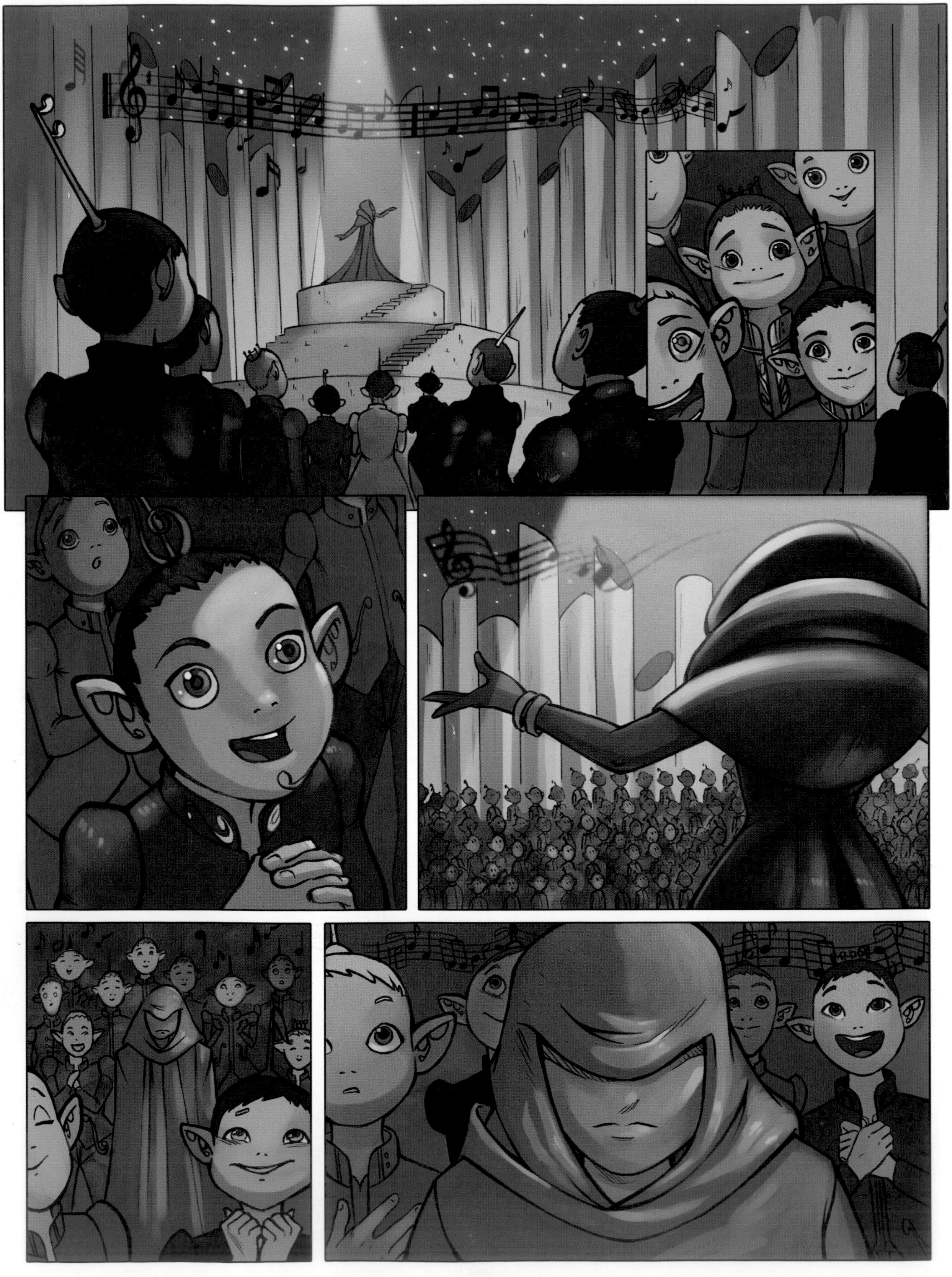

EUPHONY!

EUPHONY!

EUPHONY!

PLEASE, JUST ONE LITTLE AUTOGRAPH!

YOU WERE AWESOME THIS EVENING, EUPHONY, AS ALWAYS!

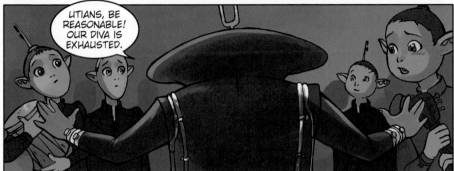

UTIANS, BE REASONABLE! OUR DIVA IS EXHAUSTED.

WHAT'S THIS...?

A ROSE? HERE? WHO WOULD DARE...

HEY, YOU! WAIT!

SEVERAL MONTHS LATER...

WHEW! AFTER THE PLANET OF THE FIREBIRD, IT'S NICE TO FIND A QUIET TOWN.

AND WITH ANY LUCK, THEY'LL HAVE A GOOD BUTCHER.

HA HA! WHAT'S YOUR SECRET, FOX? WE'VE BEEN CHASING THE SNAKE AROUND THE ENTIRE UNIVERSE AND ALL YOU THINK ABOUT IS EATING.

DOESN'T ANYTHING ELSE MATTER TO YOU?

WHAT ABOUT MUSIC? I'VE ALWAYS DREAMED OF SINGING FOR MY ROSE.

AAAARRRGH!

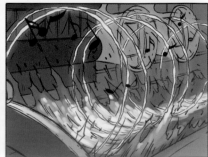

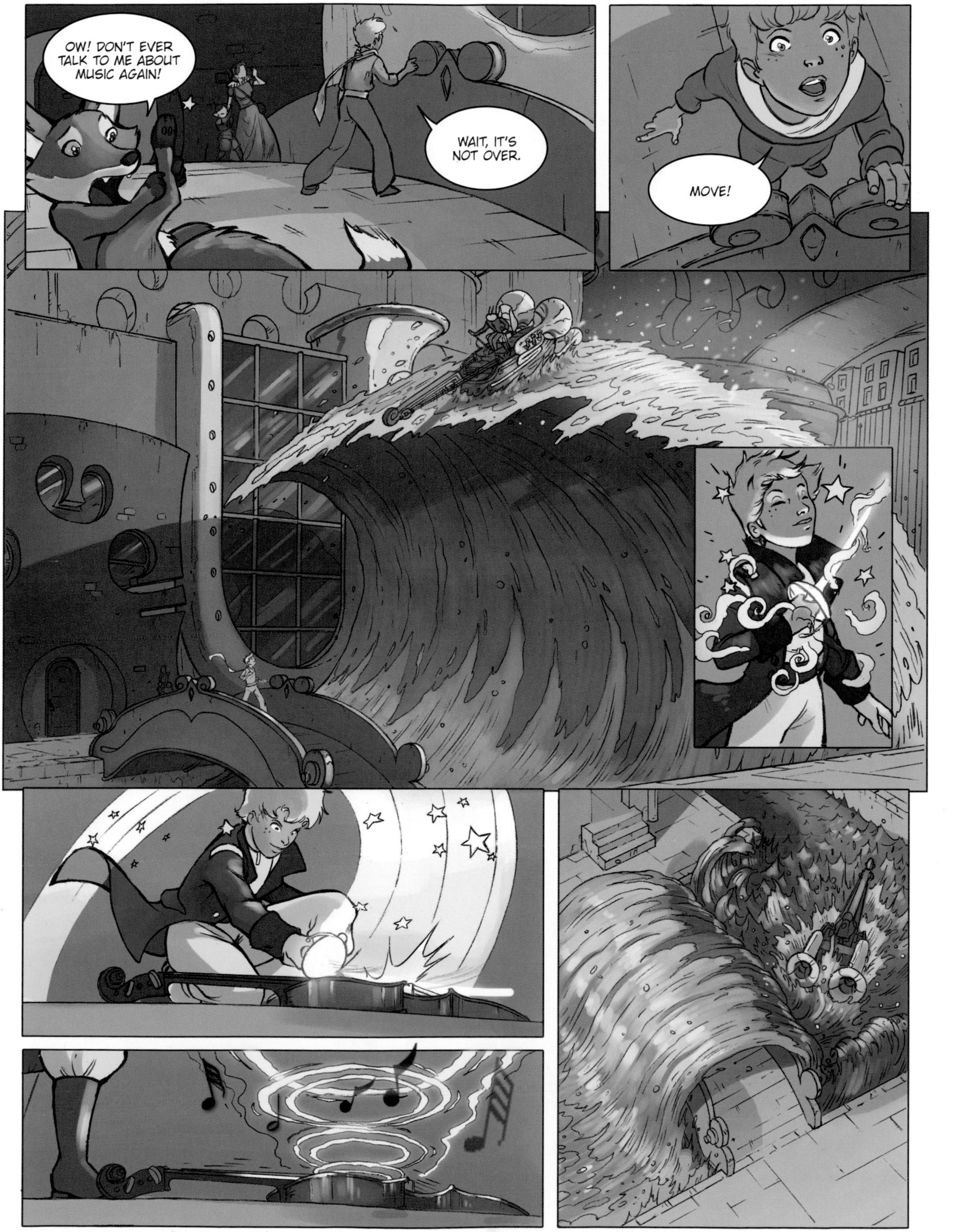
OW! DON'T EVER TALK TO ME ABOUT MUSIC AGAIN!
WAIT, IT'S NOT OVER.
MOVE!

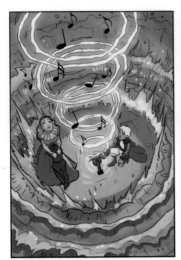

GOOD THING YOU HAD THAT VIOLIN WITH YOU!

FOX?

COFF COFF COFF...I... COFF...

GOOD FOR YOU! IT LOOKS LIKE YOU'VE FOUND A NEW FRIEND.

COFF... WHO...WHO ARE YOU?

OF COURSE, LITTLE PRINCE. I'VE DECIDED TO BECOME A HERO LIKE YOU. I SHOULD GET DINNER AS A REWARD.

WHAT ARE YOU TALKING ABOUT? I DIDN'T NEED YOUR HELP, YOU GRUBBY TOMCAT!

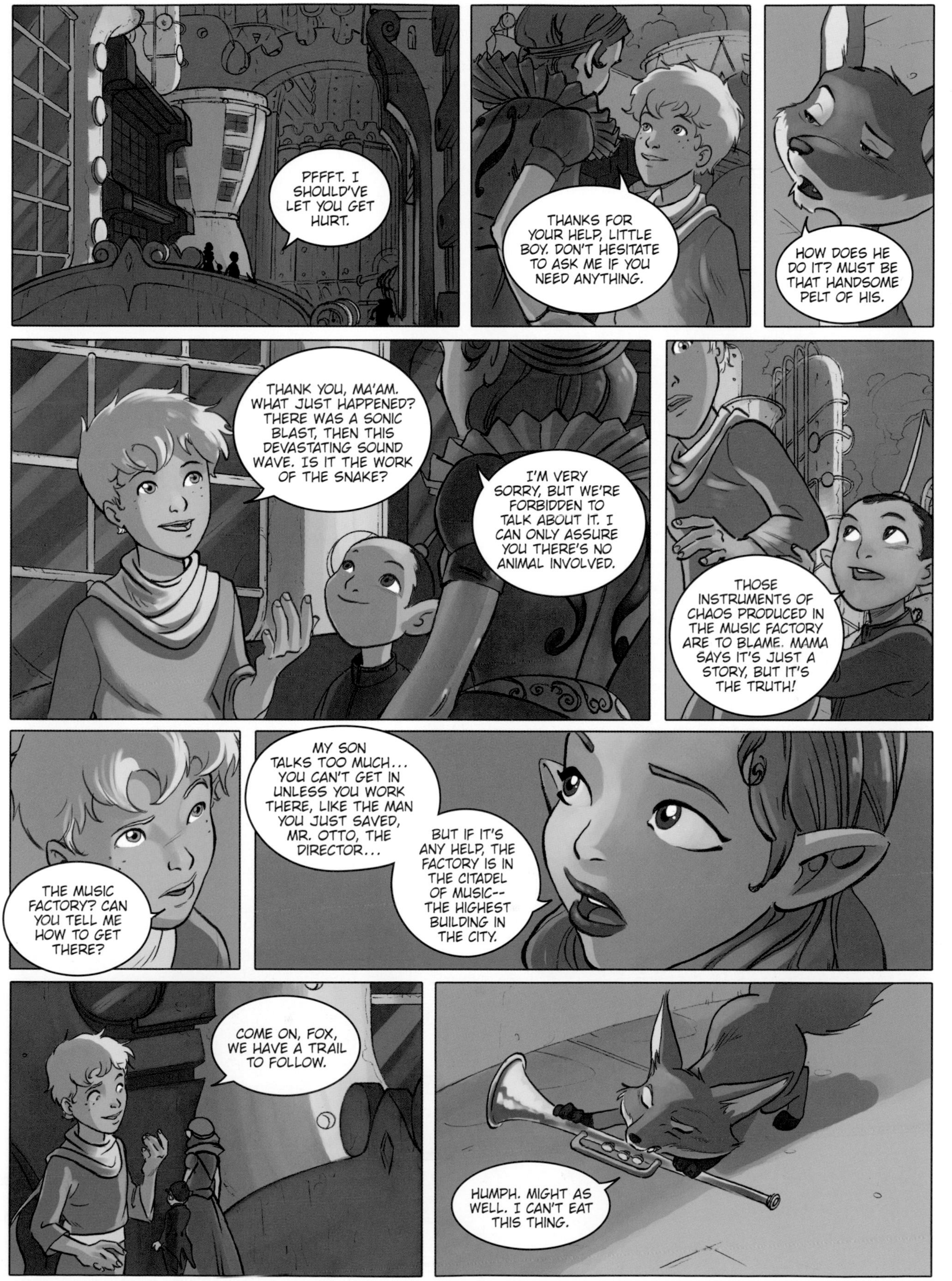
PFFFT. I SHOULD'VE LET YOU GET HURT.
THANKS FOR YOUR HELP, LITTLE BOY. DON'T HESITATE TO ASK ME IF YOU NEED ANYTHING.
HOW DOES HE DO IT? MUST BE THAT HANDSOME PELT OF HIS.
THANK YOU, MA'AM. WHAT JUST HAPPENED? THERE WAS A SONIC BLAST, THEN THIS DEVASTATING SOUND WAVE. IS IT THE WORK OF THE SNAKE?
I'M VERY SORRY, BUT WE'RE FORBIDDEN TO TALK ABOUT IT. I CAN ONLY ASSURE YOU THERE'S NO ANIMAL INVOLVED.
THOSE INSTRUMENTS OF CHAOS PRODUCED IN THE MUSIC FACTORY ARE TO BLAME. MAMA SAYS IT'S JUST A STORY, BUT IT'S THE TRUTH!
THE MUSIC FACTORY? CAN YOU TELL ME HOW TO GET THERE?
MY SON TALKS TOO MUCH... YOU CAN'T GET IN UNLESS YOU WORK THERE, LIKE THE MAN YOU JUST SAVED, MR. OTTO, THE DIRECTOR...
BUT IF IT'S ANY HELP, THE FACTORY IS IN THE CITADEL OF MUSIC-- THE HIGHEST BUILDING IN THE CITY.
COME ON, FOX, WE HAVE A TRAIL TO FOLLOW.
HUMPH. MIGHT AS WELL. I CAN'T EAT THIS THING.

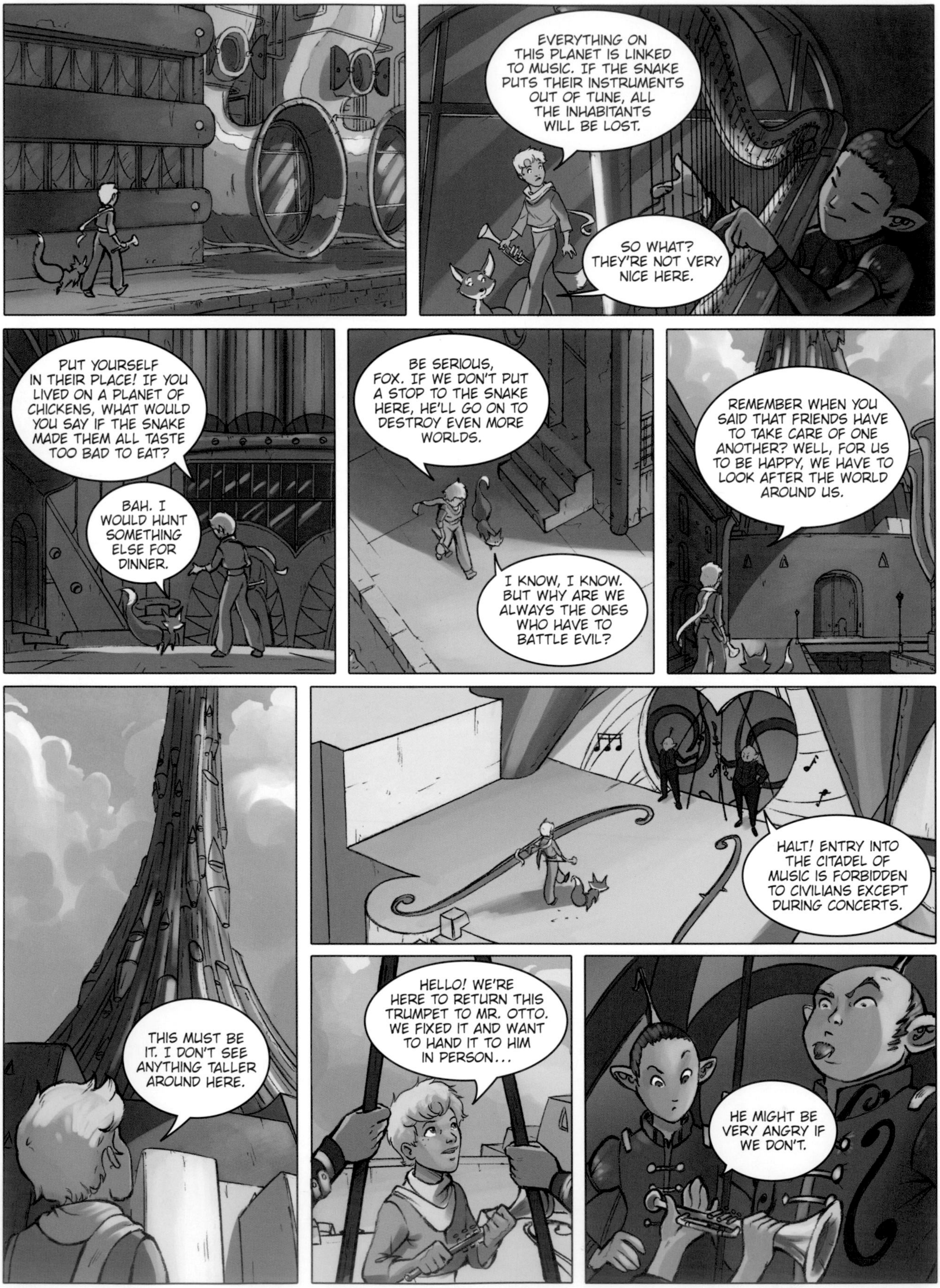
EVERYTHING ON THIS PLANET IS LINKED TO MUSIC. IF THE SNAKE PUTS THEIR INSTRUMENTS OUT OF TUNE, ALL THE INHABITANTS WILL BE LOST.
SO WHAT? THEY'RE NOT VERY NICE HERE.
PUT YOURSELF IN THEIR PLACE! IF YOU LIVED ON A PLANET OF CHICKENS, WHAT WOULD YOU SAY IF THE SNAKE MADE THEM ALL TASTE TOO BAD TO EAT?
BAH. I WOULD HUNT SOMETHING ELSE FOR DINNER.
BE SERIOUS, FOX. IF WE DON'T PUT A STOP TO THE SNAKE HERE, HE'LL GO ON TO DESTROY EVEN MORE WORLDS.
I KNOW, I KNOW. BUT WHY ARE WE ALWAYS THE ONES WHO HAVE TO BATTLE EVIL?
REMEMBER WHEN YOU SAID THAT FRIENDS HAVE TO TAKE CARE OF ONE ANOTHER? WELL, FOR US TO BE HAPPY, WE HAVE TO LOOK AFTER THE WORLD AROUND US.
THIS MUST BE IT. I DON'T SEE ANYTHING TALLER AROUND HERE.
HALT! ENTRY INTO THE CITADEL OF MUSIC IS FORBIDDEN TO CIVILIANS EXCEPT DURING CONCERTS.
HELLO! WE'RE HERE TO RETURN THIS TRUMPET TO MR. OTTO. WE FIXED IT AND WANT TO HAND IT TO HIM IN PERSON...
HE MIGHT BE VERY ANGRY IF WE DON'T.

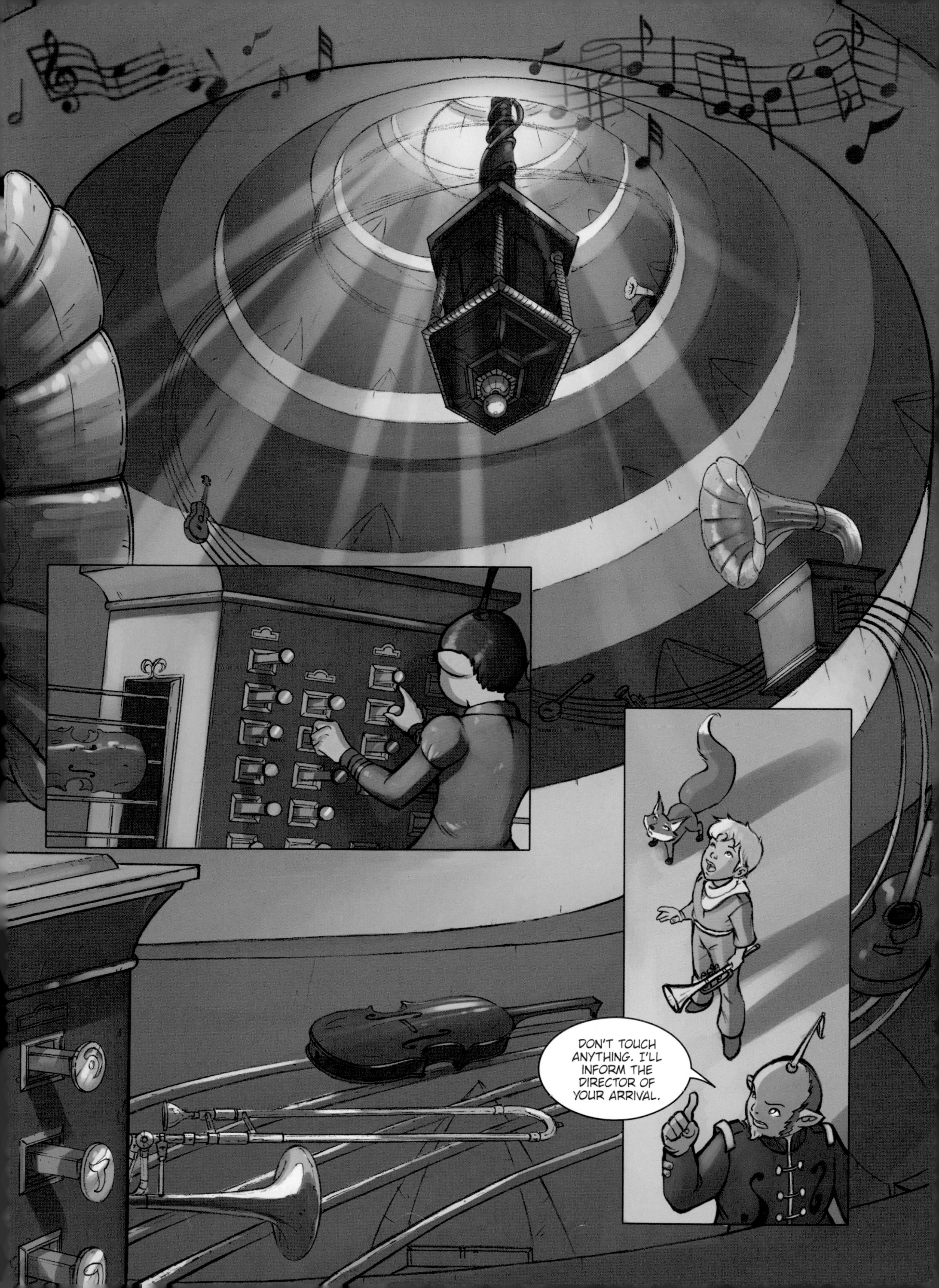
DON'T TOUCH ANYTHING. I'LL INFORM THE DIRECTOR OF YOUR ARRIVAL.

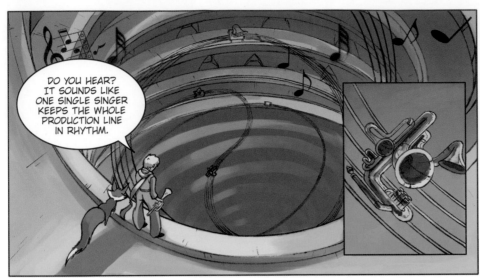

DO YOU HEAR? IT SOUNDS LIKE ONE SINGLE SINGER KEEPS THE WHOLE PRODUCTION LINE IN RHYTHM.

HEY, LOOK AT THAT. ISN'T IT STRANGE?

MAYBE IT'S ONE OF THOSE INSTRUMENTS OF CHAOS WE HEARD ABOUT! LET'S FOLLOW IT!

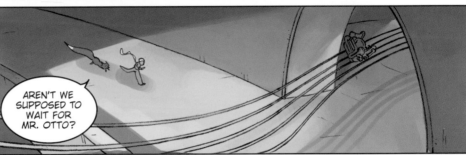

AREN'T WE SUPPOSED TO WAIT FOR MR. OTTO?

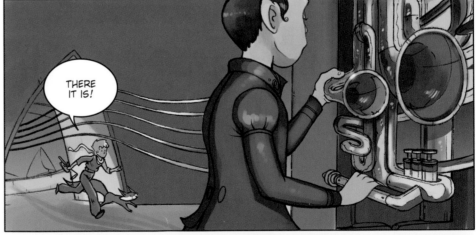

THERE IT IS!

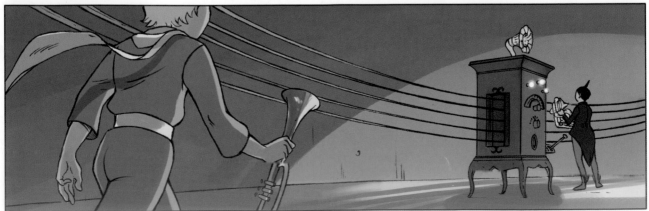

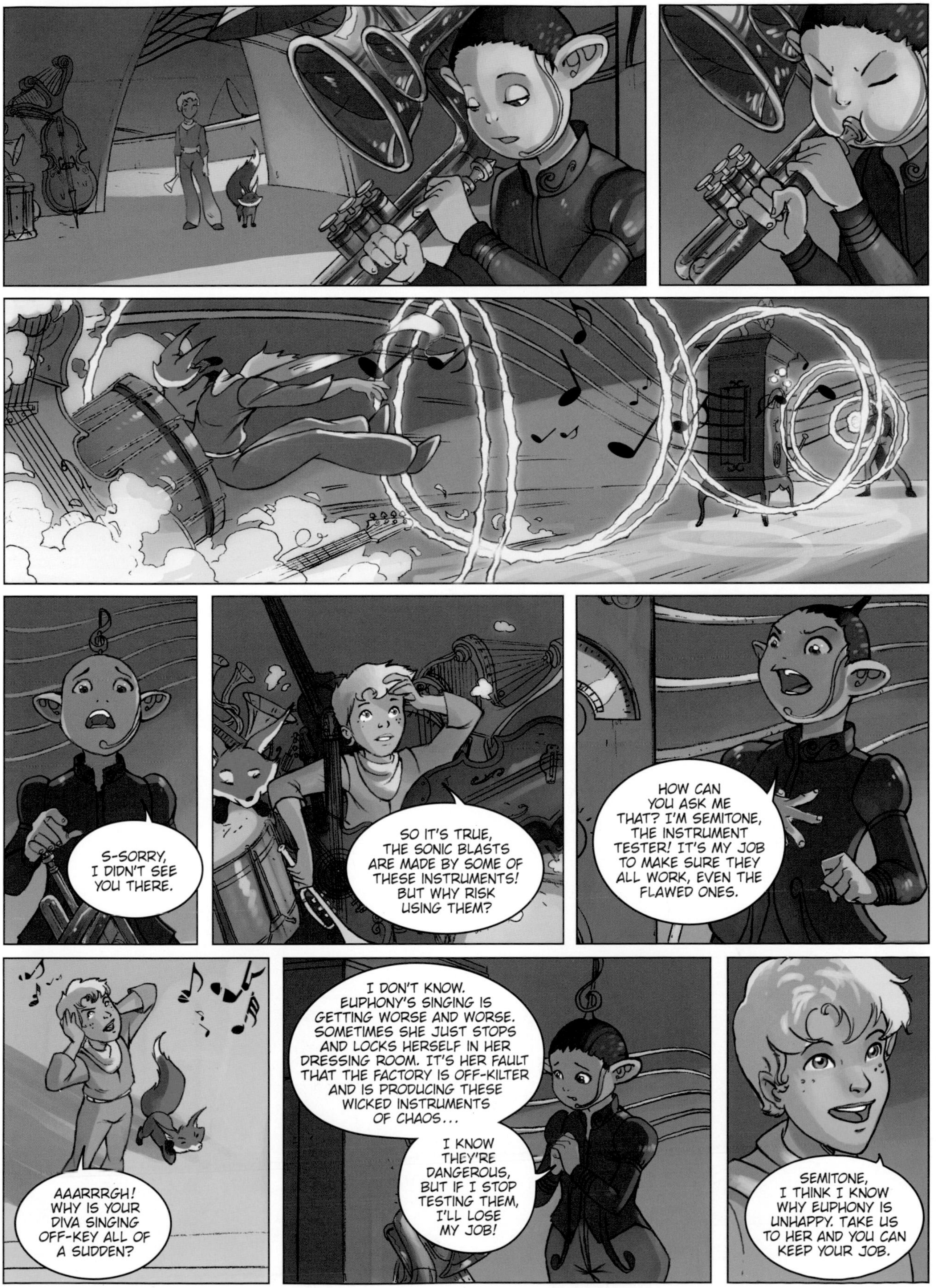
S-SORRY, I DIDN'T SEE YOU THERE.
SO IT'S TRUE, THE SONIC BLASTS ARE MADE BY SOME OF THESE INSTRUMENTS! BUT WHY RISK USING THEM?
HOW CAN YOU ASK ME THAT? I'M SEMITONE, THE INSTRUMENT TESTER! IT'S MY JOB TO MAKE SURE THEY ALL WORK, EVEN THE FLAWED ONES.
AAARRRGH! WHY IS YOUR DIVA SINGING OFF-KEY ALL OF A SUDDEN?
I DON'T KNOW. EUPHONY'S SINGING IS GETTING WORSE AND WORSE. SOMETIMES SHE JUST STOPS AND LOCKS HERSELF IN HER DRESSING ROOM. IT'S HER FAULT THAT THE FACTORY IS OFF-KILTER AND IS PRODUCING THESE WICKED INSTRUMENTS OF CHAOS...
I KNOW THEY'RE DANGEROUS, BUT IF I STOP TESTING THEM, I'LL LOSE MY JOB!
SEMITONE, I THINK I KNOW WHY EUPHONY IS UNHAPPY. TAKE US TO HER AND YOU CAN KEEP YOUR JOB.

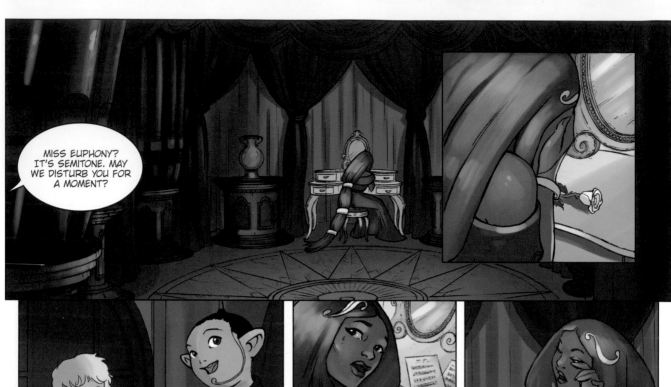

MISS EUPHONY? IT'S SEMITONE. MAY WE DISTURB YOU FOR A MOMENT?

THIS IS THE LITTLE PRINCE AND HIS FRIEND FOX. THEY MAY HAVE GOOD NEWS ABOUT YOUR VOICE...

WHAT? NO...

WHO LET YOU IN? I...I NEED TO FOCUS. YOU'LL HAVE TO WAIT FOR MY NEXT CONCERT TO GET AN AUTOGRAPH.

EUPHONY, SEMITONE TOLD US EVERYTHING. WE'RE BIG FANS OF YOURS, AND WE WANT TO EASE YOUR WORRIES.

AND WHAT COULD YOU POSSIBLY DO FOR ME, LITTLE PRINCE?

I KNOW THAT A SNAKE HAS CONTACTED YOU, EUPHONY. HE MUST HAVE FOUND YOU WHEN YOU HAD A MOMENT OF WEAKNESS, SO HE COULD DISTURB YOUR SINGING. BUT YOU DON'T HAVE TO LISTEN TO HIS FALSE PROMISES OF HAPPINESS. HIS ONLY GOAL IS TO DESTROY YOUR WORLD.

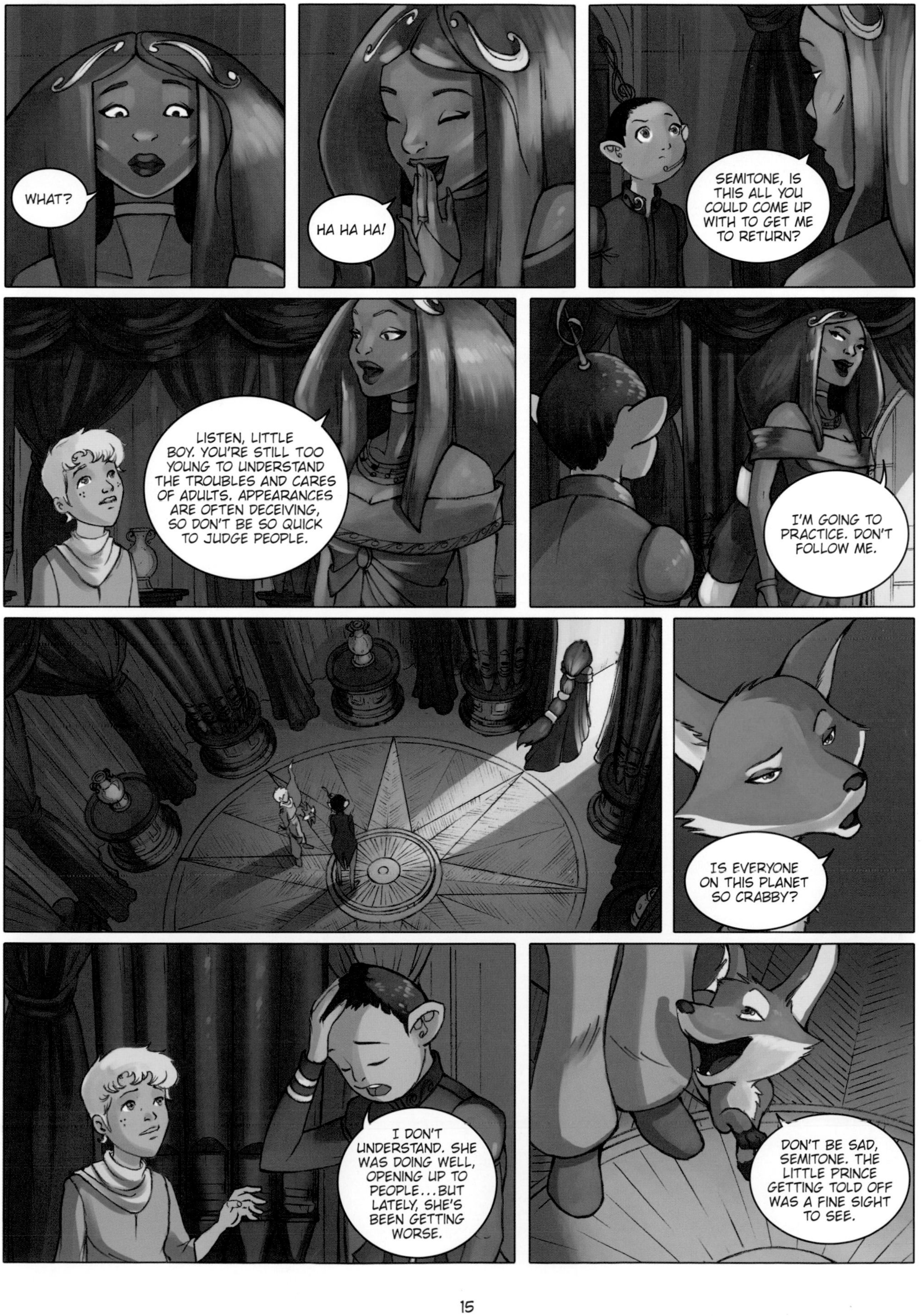
WHAT?
HA HA HA!
SEMITONE, IS THIS ALL YOU COULD COME UP WITH TO GET ME TO RETURN?
LISTEN, LITTLE BOY. YOU'RE STILL TOO YOUNG TO UNDERSTAND THE TROUBLES AND CARES OF ADULTS. APPEARANCES ARE OFTEN DECEIVING, SO DON'T BE SO QUICK TO JUDGE PEOPLE.
I'M GOING TO PRACTICE. DON'T FOLLOW ME.
IS EVERYONE ON THIS PLANET SO CRABBY?
I DON'T UNDERSTAND. SHE WAS DOING WELL, OPENING UP TO PEOPLE...BUT LATELY, SHE'S BEEN GETTING WORSE.
DON'T BE SAD, SEMITONE. THE LITTLE PRINCE GETTING TOLD OFF WAS A FINE SIGHT TO SEE.

I KNOW HOW TO RESCUE YOUR FACTORY! I'LL SING IN EUPHONY'S PLACE.

UM...I DON'T KNOW IF THAT'S A GOOD IDEA, LITTLE PRINCE. SHOULDN'T WE STICK TO LOOKING FOR THE SNAKE?

TOO LATE! THIS PLANET IS DOOMED!

URG! STOP!

THANKS FOR THE OFFER, LITTLE PRINCE, BUT I THINK WE'LL KEEP OUR DIVA...

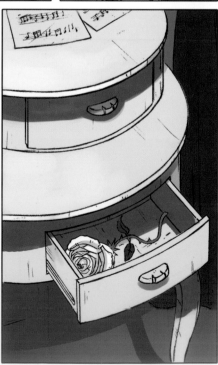

BUT-- WHAT...?

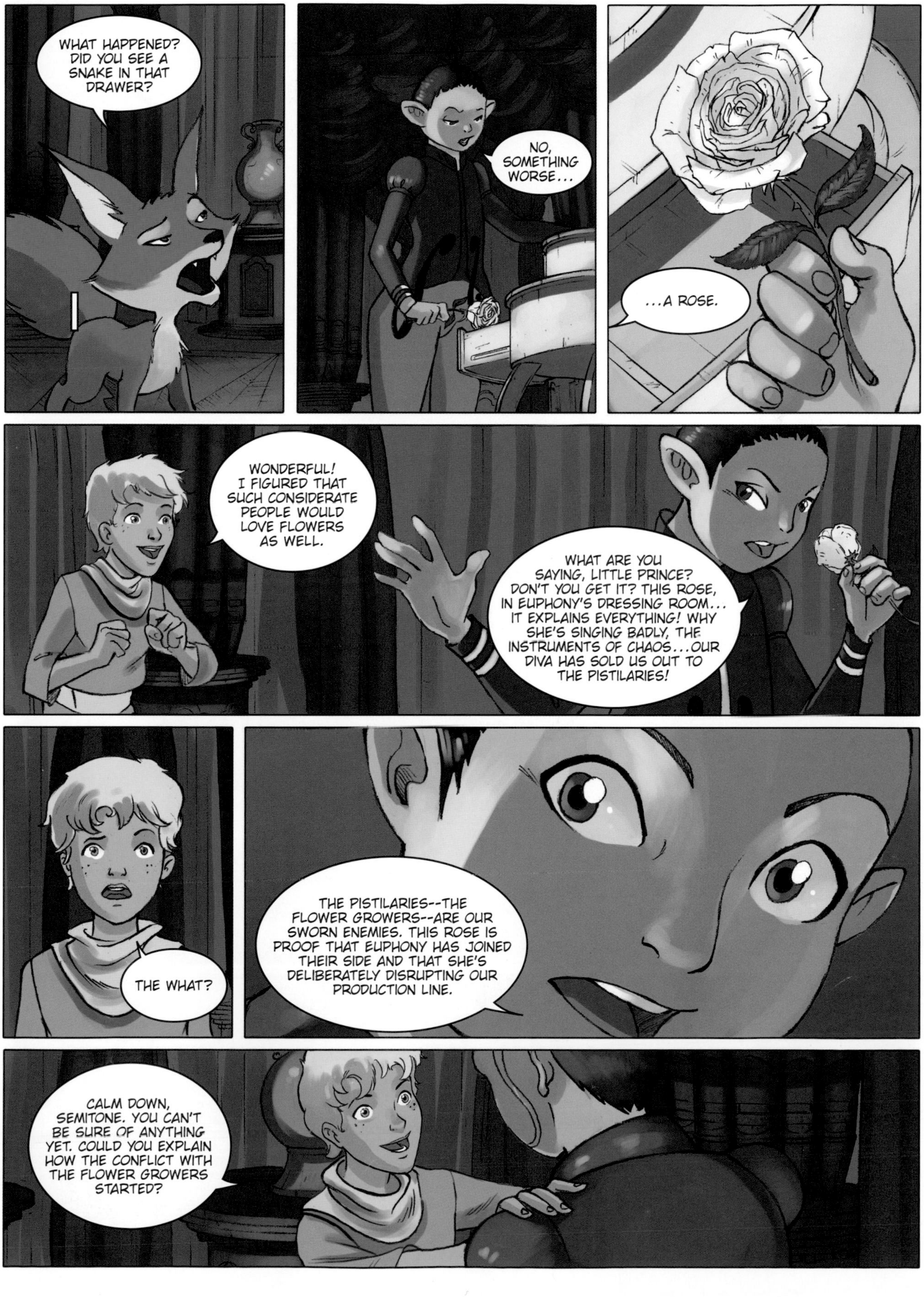
WHAT HAPPENED? DID YOU SEE A SNAKE IN THAT DRAWER?
NO, SOMETHING WORSE...
...A ROSE.
WONDERFUL! I FIGURED THAT SUCH CONSIDERATE PEOPLE WOULD LOVE FLOWERS AS WELL.
WHAT ARE YOU SAYING, LITTLE PRINCE? DON'T YOU GET IT? THIS ROSE, IN EUPHONY'S DRESSING ROOM... IT EXPLAINS EVERYTHING! WHY SHE'S SINGING BADLY, THE INSTRUMENTS OF CHAOS...OUR DIVA HAS SOLD US OUT TO THE PISTILARIES!
THE WHAT?
THE PISTILARIES--THE FLOWER GROWERS--ARE OUR SWORN ENEMIES. THIS ROSE IS PROOF THAT EUPHONY HAS JOINED THEIR SIDE AND THAT SHE'S DELIBERATELY DISRUPTING OUR PRODUCTION LINE.
CALM DOWN, SEMITONE. YOU CAN'T BE SURE OF ANYTHING YET. COULD YOU EXPLAIN HOW THE CONFLICT WITH THE FLOWER GROWERS STARTED?

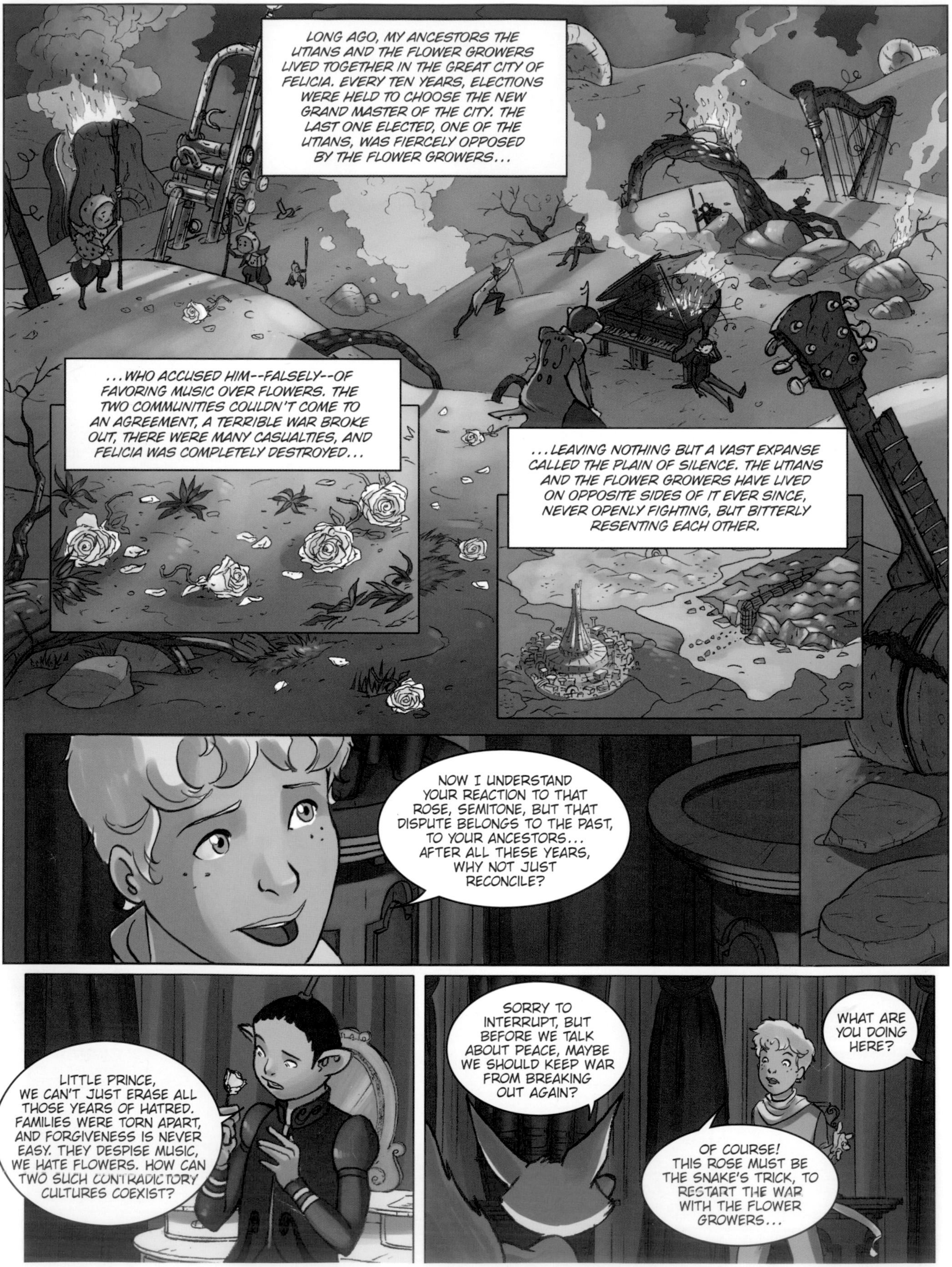
LONG AGO, MY ANCESTORS THE UTIANS AND THE FLOWER GROWERS LIVED TOGETHER IN THE GREAT CITY OF FELICIA. EVERY TEN YEARS, ELECTIONS WERE HELD TO CHOOSE THE NEW GRAND MASTER OF THE CITY. THE LAST ONE ELECTED, ONE OF THE UTIANS, WAS FIERCELY OPPOSED BY THE FLOWER GROWERS...
...WHO ACCUSED HIM--FALSELY--OF FAVORING MUSIC OVER FLOWERS. THE TWO COMMUNITIES COULDN'T COME TO AN AGREEMENT, A TERRIBLE WAR BROKE OUT, THERE WERE MANY CASUALTIES, AND FELICIA WAS COMPLETELY DESTROYED...
...LEAVING NOTHING BUT A VAST EXPANSE CALLED THE PLAIN OF SILENCE. THE UTIANS AND THE FLOWER GROWERS HAVE LIVED ON OPPOSITE SIDES OF IT EVER SINCE, NEVER OPENLY FIGHTING, BUT BITTERLY RESENTING EACH OTHER.
NOW I UNDERSTAND YOUR REACTION TO THAT ROSE, SEMITONE, BUT THAT DISPUTE BELONGS TO THE PAST, TO YOUR ANCESTORS... AFTER ALL THESE YEARS, WHY NOT JUST RECONCILE?
LITTLE PRINCE, WE CAN'T JUST ERASE ALL THOSE YEARS OF HATRED. FAMILIES WERE TORN APART, AND FORGIVENESS IS NEVER EASY. THEY DESPISE MUSIC, WE HATE FLOWERS. HOW CAN TWO SUCH CONTRADICTORY CULTURES COEXIST?
SORRY TO INTERRUPT, BUT BEFORE WE TALK ABOUT PEACE, MAYBE WE SHOULD KEEP WAR FROM BREAKING OUT AGAIN?
WHAT ARE YOU DOING HERE?
OF COURSE! THIS ROSE MUST BE THE SNAKE'S TRICK, TO RESTART THE WAR WITH THE FLOWER GROWERS...

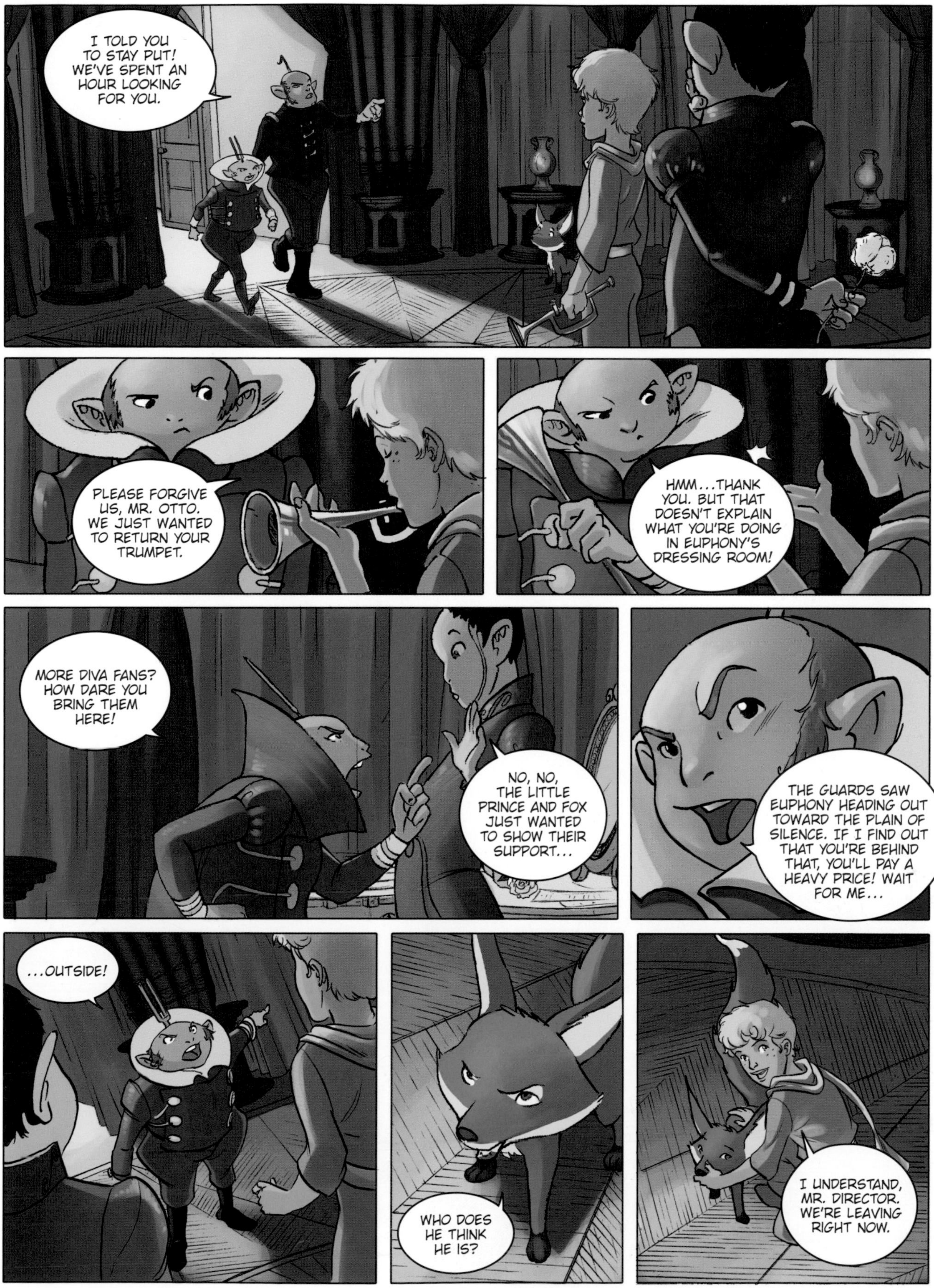
I TOLD YOU TO STAY PUT! WE'VE SPENT AN HOUR LOOKING FOR YOU.
PLEASE FORGIVE US, MR. OTTO. WE JUST WANTED TO RETURN YOUR TRUMPET.
HMM...THANK YOU. BUT THAT DOESN'T EXPLAIN WHAT YOU'RE DOING IN EUPHONY'S DRESSING ROOM!
MORE DIVA FANS? HOW DARE YOU BRING THEM HERE!
NO, NO, THE LITTLE PRINCE AND FOX JUST WANTED TO SHOW THEIR SUPPORT...
THE GUARDS SAW EUPHONY HEADING OUT TOWARD THE PLAIN OF SILENCE. IF I FIND OUT THAT YOU'RE BEHIND THAT, YOU'LL PAY A HEAVY PRICE! WAIT FOR ME...
...OUTSIDE!
WHO DOES HE THINK HE IS?
I UNDERSTAND, MR. DIRECTOR. WE'RE LEAVING RIGHT NOW.

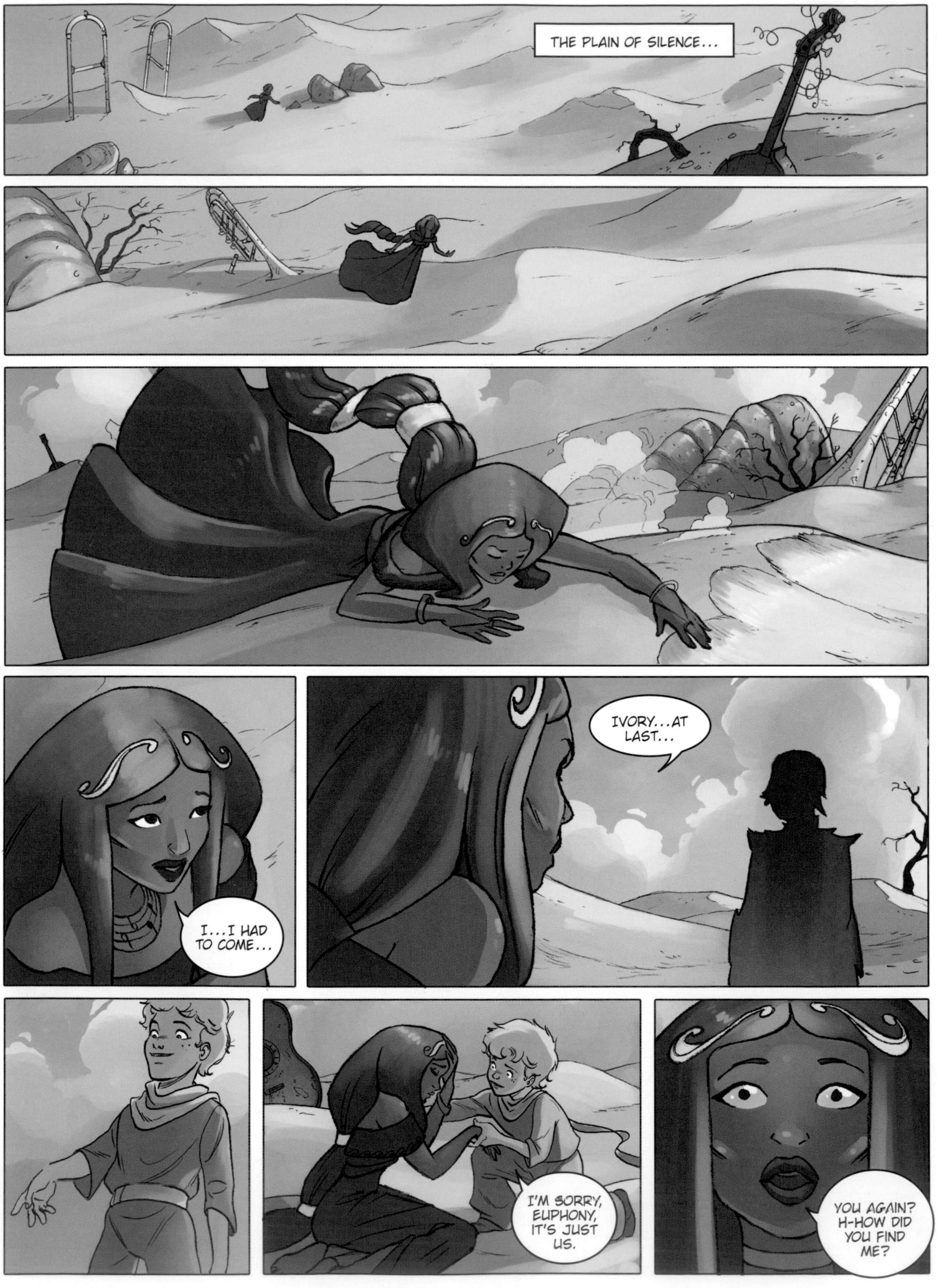
THE PLAIN OF SILENCE...
I...I HAD TO COME...
IVORY...AT LAST...
I'M SORRY, EUPHONY, IT'S JUST US.
YOU AGAIN? H-HOW DID YOU FIND ME?

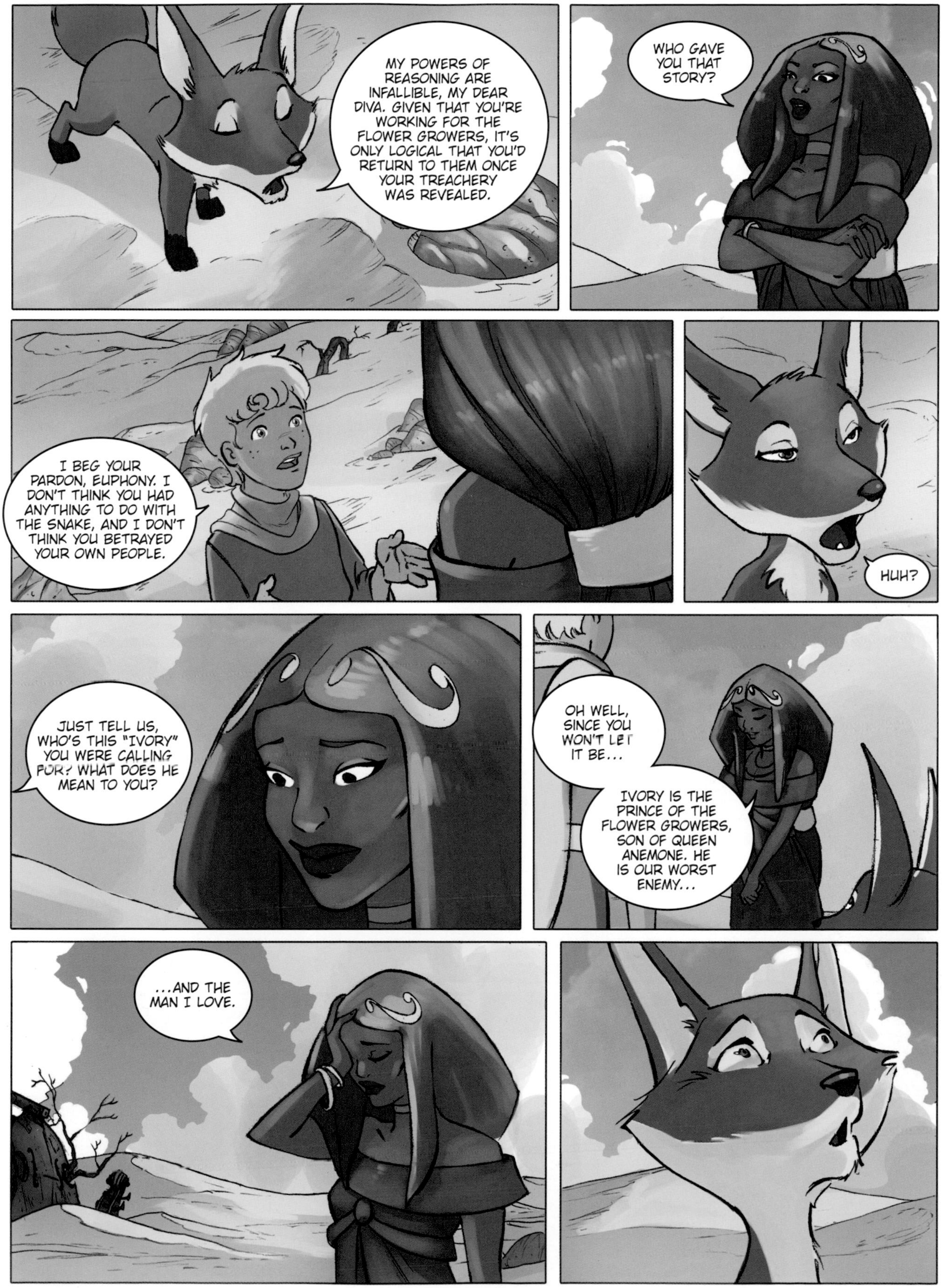
MY POWERS OF REASONING ARE INFALLIBLE, MY DEAR DIVA. GIVEN THAT YOU'RE WORKING FOR THE FLOWER GROWERS, IT'S ONLY LOGICAL THAT YOU'D RETURN TO THEM ONCE YOUR TREACHERY WAS REVEALED.
WHO GAVE YOU THAT STORY?
I BEG YOUR PARDON, EUPHONY. I DON'T THINK YOU HAD ANYTHING TO DO WITH THE SNAKE, AND I DON'T THINK YOU BETRAYED YOUR OWN PEOPLE.
HUH?
JUST TELL US, WHO'S THIS "IVORY" YOU WERE CALLING FOR? WHAT DOES HE MEAN TO YOU?
OH WELL, SINCE YOU WON'T LET IT BE...
IVORY IS THE PRINCE OF THE FLOWER GROWERS, SON OF QUEEN ANEMONE. HE IS OUR WORST ENEMY...
...AND THE MAN I LOVE.

IT ALL BEGAN SEVERAL MONTHS AGO. AN UNKNOWN MAN KEPT LEAVING ROSES IN FRONT OF MY DRESSING ROOM. AT FIRST, I THOUGHT IT WAS A CRUEL PRANK, SINCE FLOWERS ARE FORBIDDEN HERE. BUT EVENTUALLY, I WANTED TO KNOW MORE.

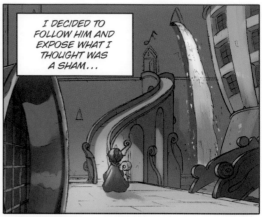

I DECIDED TO FOLLOW HIM AND EXPOSE WHAT I THOUGHT WAS A SHAM...

YOU MUSTN'T FOLLOW ME, MY DEAR DIVA...I DON'T DESERVE YOUR ATTENTION.

WHO ARE YOU? WHY DO YOU OFFER ME ROSES? DON'T YOU KNOW WHAT PEOPLE WILL THINK IF THEY FIND ROSES IN MY ROOM?

EUPHONY, I COULD NEVER CAUSE YOU THE SLIGHTEST HARM...

...I FEAR I'M NOTHING MORE THAN AN EARTHWORM IN LOVE WITH A STAR...

A FLOWER GROWER?

SINCE THE FIRST TIME I SAW YOU AND HEARD YOUR VOICE, MY WHOLE SOUL HAS BEEN YOURS, AND ALL OUR DIFFERENCES MEAN NOTHING TO ME.

EVEN THOUGH IT'S FORBIDDEN, I LOVE YOU, EUPHONY.

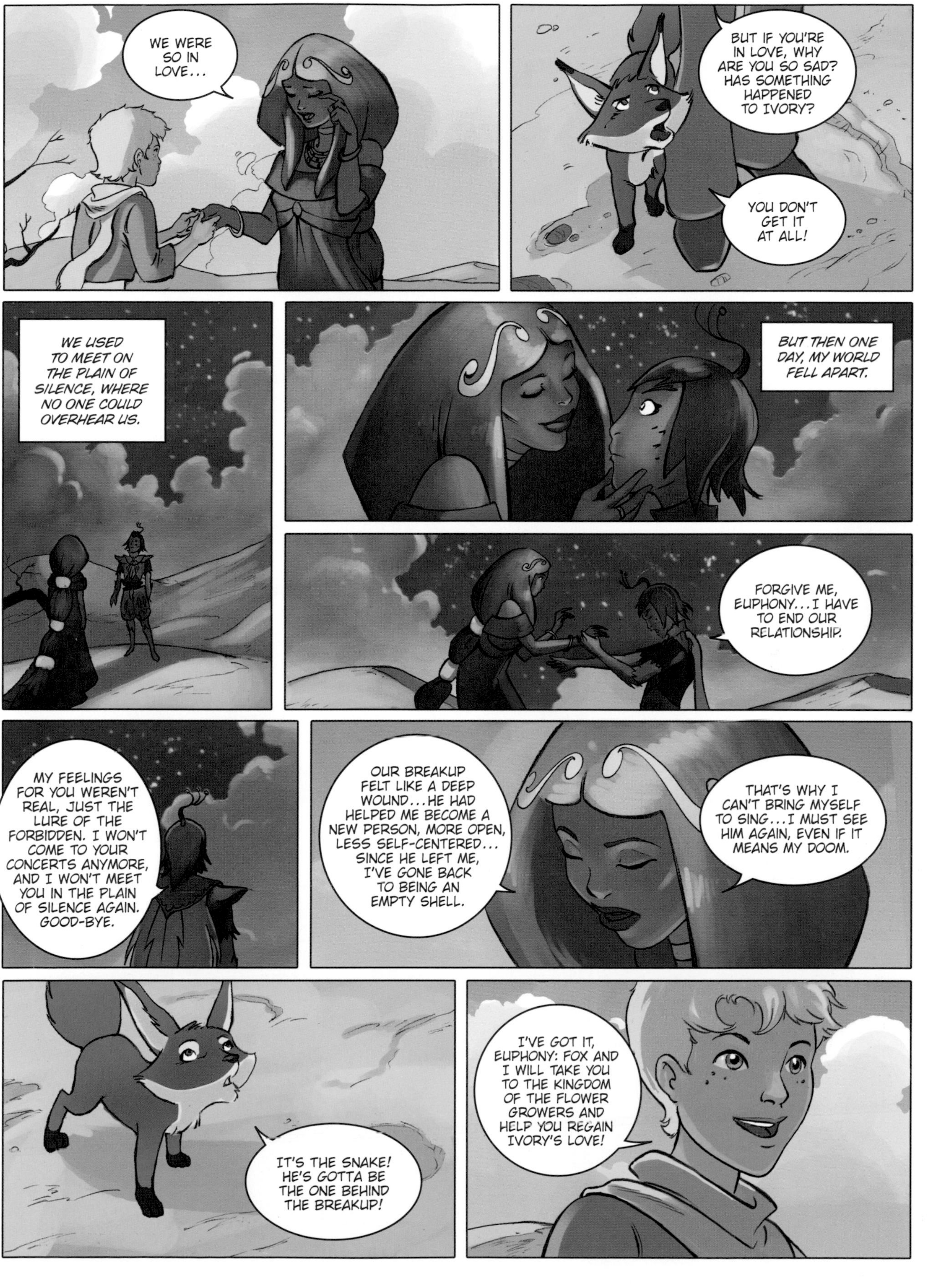

WE WERE SO IN LOVE...
BUT IF YOU'RE IN LOVE, WHY ARE YOU SO SAD? HAS SOMETHING HAPPENED TO IVORY?
YOU DON'T GET IT AT ALL!
WE USED TO MEET ON THE PLAIN OF SILENCE, WHERE NO ONE COULD OVERHEAR US.
BUT THEN ONE DAY, MY WORLD FELL APART.
FORGIVE ME, EUPHONY... I HAVE TO END OUR RELATIONSHIP.
MY FEELINGS FOR YOU WEREN'T REAL, JUST THE LURE OF THE FORBIDDEN. I WON'T COME TO YOUR CONCERTS ANYMORE, AND I WON'T MEET YOU IN THE PLAIN OF SILENCE AGAIN. GOOD-BYE.
OUR BREAKUP FELT LIKE A DEEP WOUND... HE HAD HELPED ME BECOME A NEW PERSON, MORE OPEN, LESS SELF-CENTERED... SINCE HE LEFT ME, I'VE GONE BACK TO BEING AN EMPTY SHELL.
THAT'S WHY I CAN'T BRING MYSELF TO SING... I MUST SEE HIM AGAIN, EVEN IF IT MEANS MY DOOM.
IT'S THE SNAKE! HE'S GOTTA BE THE ONE BEHIND THE BREAKUP!
I'VE GOT IT, EUPHONY: FOX AND I WILL TAKE YOU TO THE KINGDOM OF THE FLOWER GROWERS AND HELP YOU REGAIN IVORY'S LOVE!

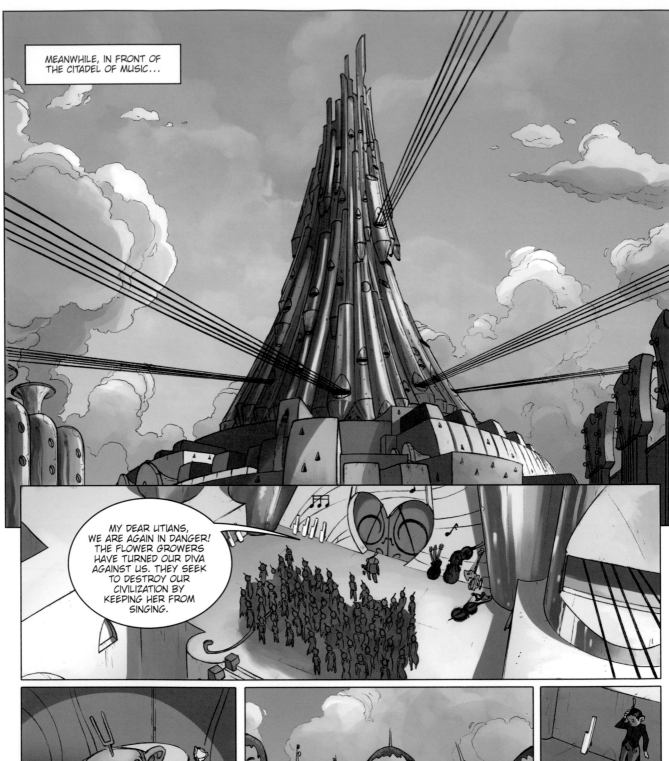

MEANWHILE, IN FRONT OF THE CITADEL OF MUSIC...

MY DEAR LITIANS, WE ARE AGAIN IN DANGER! THE FLOWER GROWERS HAVE TURNED OUR DIVA AGAINST US. THEY SEEK TO DESTROY OUR CIVILIZATION BY KEEPING HER FROM SINGING.

THIS ROSE, FOUND IN EUPHONY'S DRESSING ROOM, IS PROOF THAT SHE'S WORKING HAND IN HAND WITH OUR WORST ENEMIES.

THE ULTIMATE TREASON! NOW THAT SHE'S BEEN UNMASKED, THE TRAITOR EUPHONY HAS FLED. LET'S THANK SEMITONE FOR BRINGING THIS CONSPIRACY TO LIGHT!

THERE'S NO ALTERNATIVE BUT TO ATTACK FIRST, ARMED WITH OUR INSTRUMENTS OF CHAOS, AND WIPE OUT THE FLOWER GROWERS ONCE AND FOR ALL!

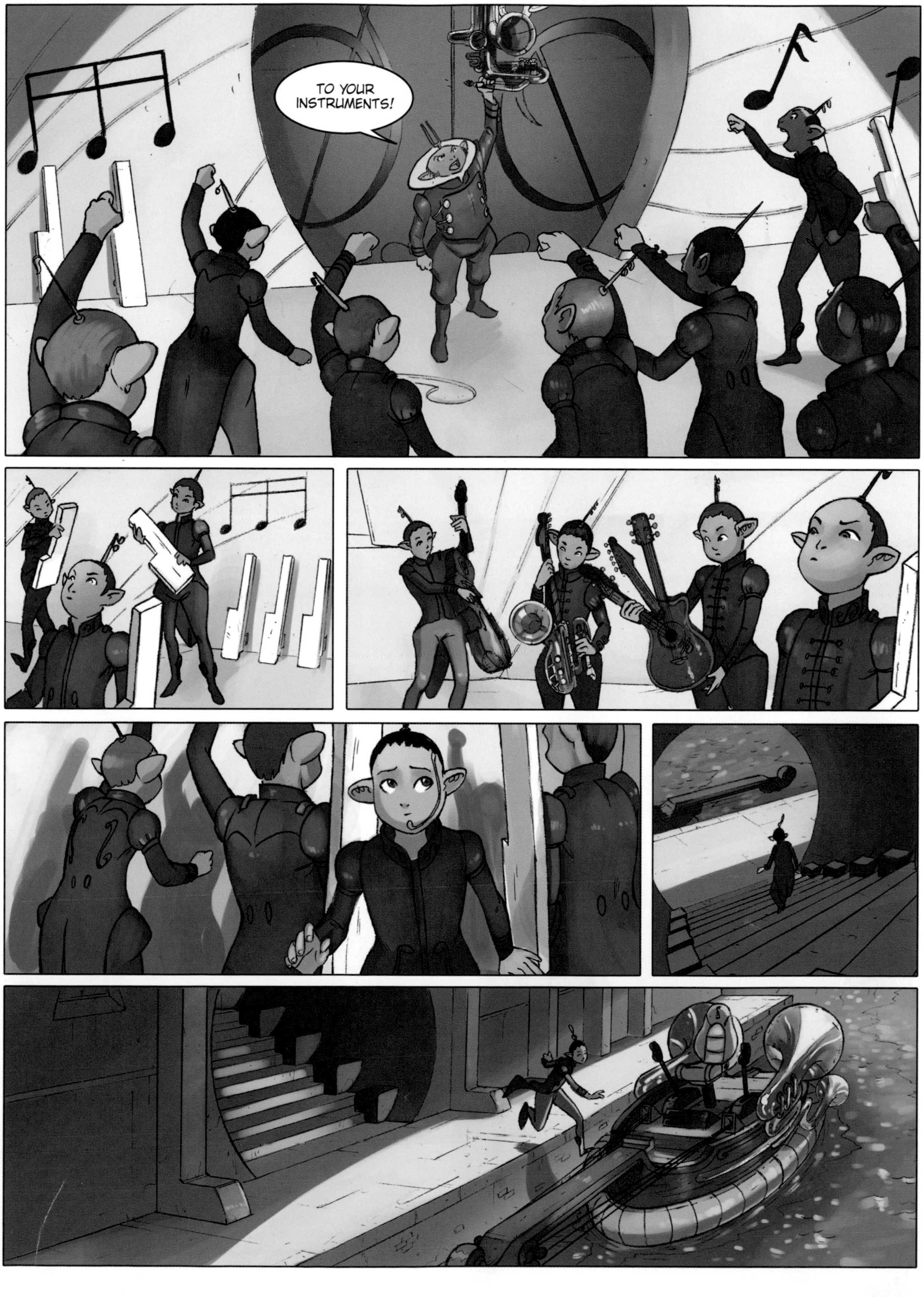
TO YOUR
INSTRUMENTS!

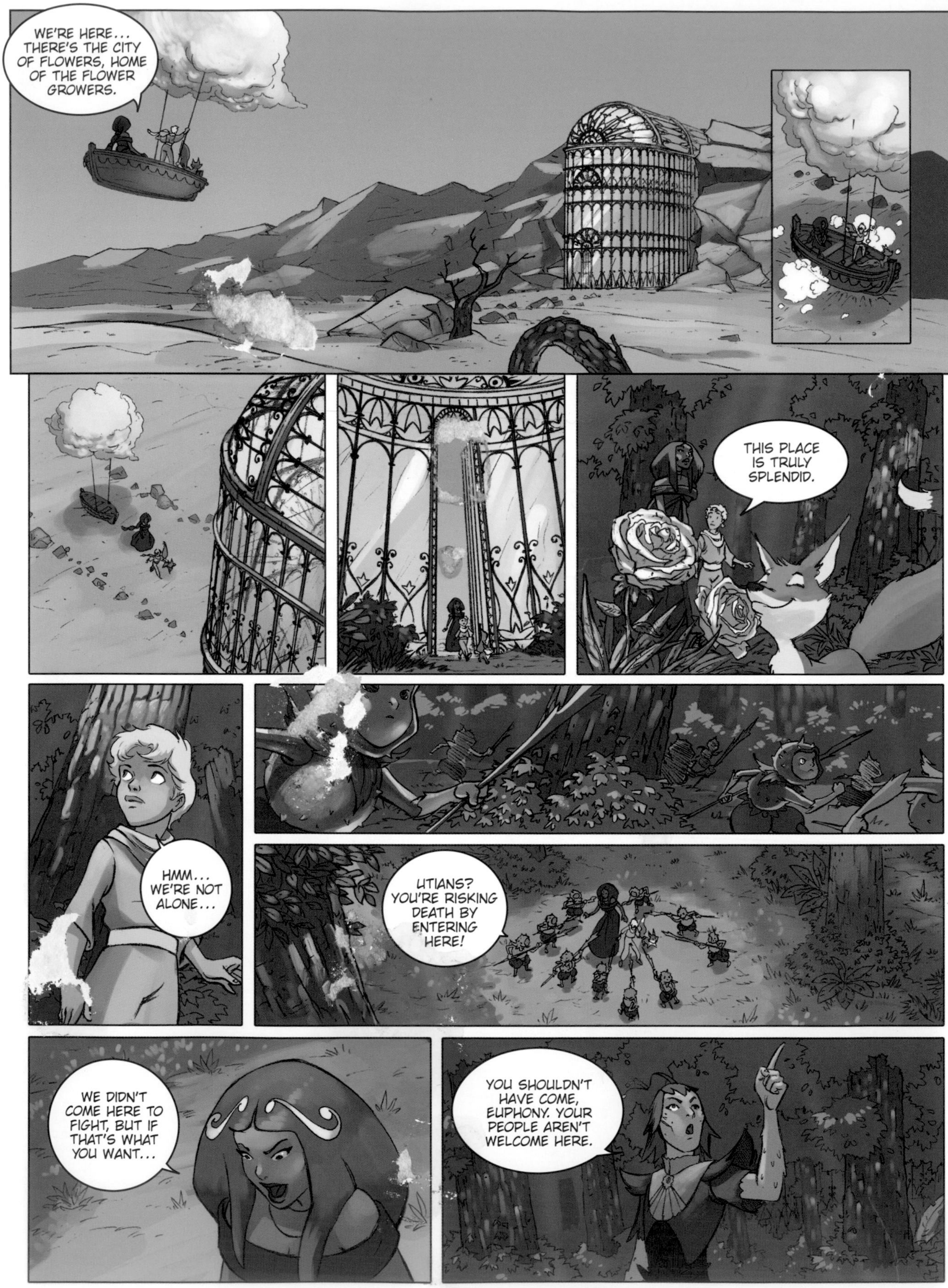
WE'RE HERE... THERE'S THE CITY OF FLOWERS, HOME OF THE FLOWER GROWERS.
THIS PLACE IS TRULY SPLENDID.
HMM... WE'RE NOT ALONE...
UTIANS? YOU'RE RISKING DEATH BY ENTERING HERE!
WE DIDN'T COME HERE TO FIGHT, BUT IF THAT'S WHAT YOU WANT...
YOU SHOULDN'T HAVE COME, EUPHONY. YOUR PEOPLE AREN'T WELCOME HERE.

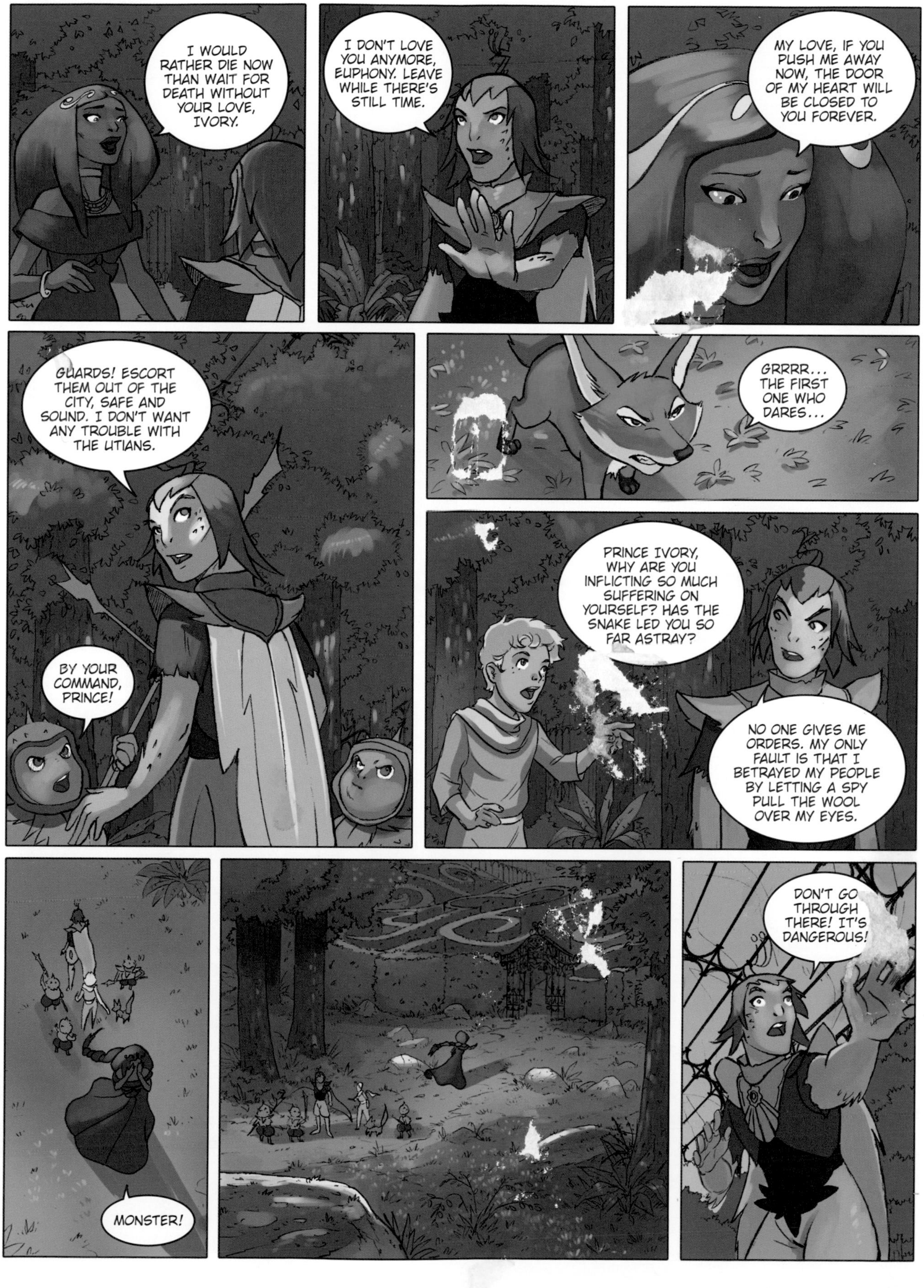

I WOULD RATHER DIE NOW THAN WAIT FOR DEATH WITHOUT YOUR LOVE, IVORY.
I DON'T LOVE YOU ANYMORE, EUPHONY. LEAVE WHILE THERE'S STILL TIME.
MY LOVE, IF YOU PUSH ME AWAY NOW, THE DOOR OF MY HEART WILL BE CLOSED TO YOU FOREVER.
GUARDS! ESCORT THEM OUT OF THE CITY, SAFE AND SOUND. I DON'T WANT ANY TROUBLE WITH THE UTIANS.
BY YOUR COMMAND, PRINCE!
GRRRR... THE FIRST ONE WHO DARES...
PRINCE IVORY, WHY ARE YOU INFLICTING SO MUCH SUFFERING ON YOURSELF? HAS THE SNAKE LED YOU SO FAR ASTRAY?
NO ONE GIVES ME ORDERS. MY ONLY FAULT IS THAT I BETRAYED MY PEOPLE BY LETTING A SPY PULL THE WOOL OVER MY EYES.
MONSTER!
DON'T GO THROUGH THERE! IT'S DANGEROUS!

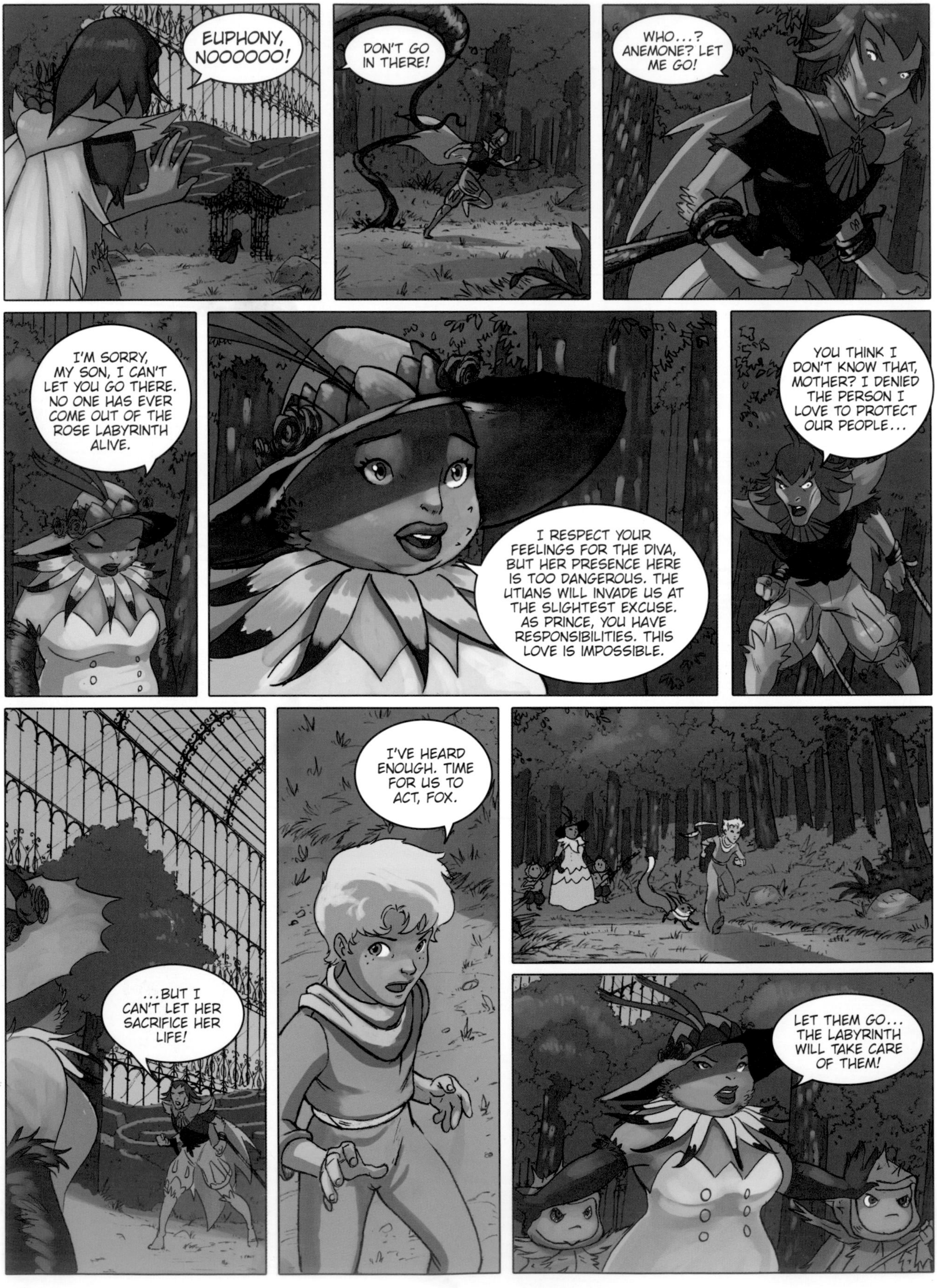
EUPHONY, NOOOOOO!
DON'T GO IN THERE!
WHO...? ANEMONE? LET ME GO!
I'M SORRY, MY SON, I CAN'T LET YOU GO THERE. NO ONE HAS EVER COME OUT OF THE ROSE LABYRINTH ALIVE.
I RESPECT YOUR FEELINGS FOR THE DIVA, BUT HER PRESENCE HERE IS TOO DANGEROUS. THE UTIANS WILL INVADE US AT THE SLIGHTEST EXCUSE. AS PRINCE, YOU HAVE RESPONSIBILITIES. THIS LOVE IS IMPOSSIBLE.
YOU THINK I DON'T KNOW THAT, MOTHER? I DENIED THE PERSON I LOVE TO PROTECT OUR PEOPLE...
...BUT I CAN'T LET HER SACRIFICE HER LIFE!
I'VE HEARD ENOUGH. TIME FOR US TO ACT, FOX.
LET THEM GO... THE LABYRINTH WILL TAKE CARE OF THEM!

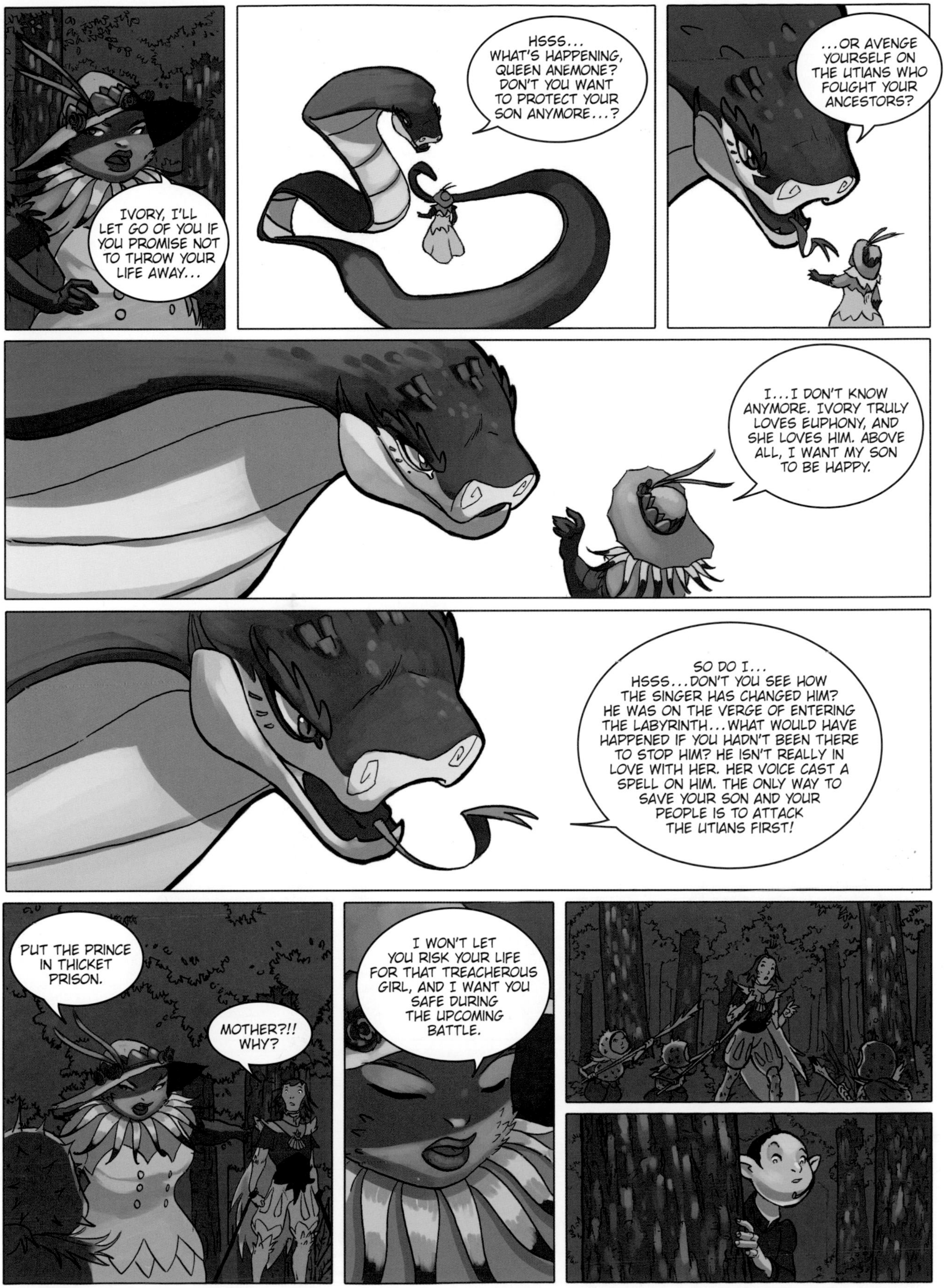
IVORY, I'LL LET GO OF YOU IF YOU PROMISE NOT TO THROW YOUR LIFE AWAY...
HSSS... WHAT'S HAPPENING, QUEEN ANEMONE? DON'T YOU WANT TO PROTECT YOUR SON ANYMORE...?
...OR AVENGE YOURSELF ON THE UTIANS WHO FOUGHT YOUR ANCESTORS?
I...I DON'T KNOW ANYMORE. IVORY TRULY LOVES EUPHONY, AND SHE LOVES HIM. ABOVE ALL, I WANT MY SON TO BE HAPPY.
SO DO I... HSSS...DON'T YOU SEE HOW THE SINGER HAS CHANGED HIM? HE WAS ON THE VERGE OF ENTERING THE LABYRINTH...WHAT WOULD HAVE HAPPENED IF YOU HADN'T BEEN THERE TO STOP HIM? HE ISN'T REALLY IN LOVE WITH HER. HER VOICE CAST A SPELL ON HIM. THE ONLY WAY TO SAVE YOUR SON AND YOUR PEOPLE IS TO ATTACK THE UTIANS FIRST!
PUT THE PRINCE IN THICKET PRISON.
MOTHER?!! WHY?
I WON'T LET YOU RISK YOUR LIFE FOR THAT TREACHEROUS GIRL, AND I WANT YOU SAFE DURING THE UPCOMING BATTLE.

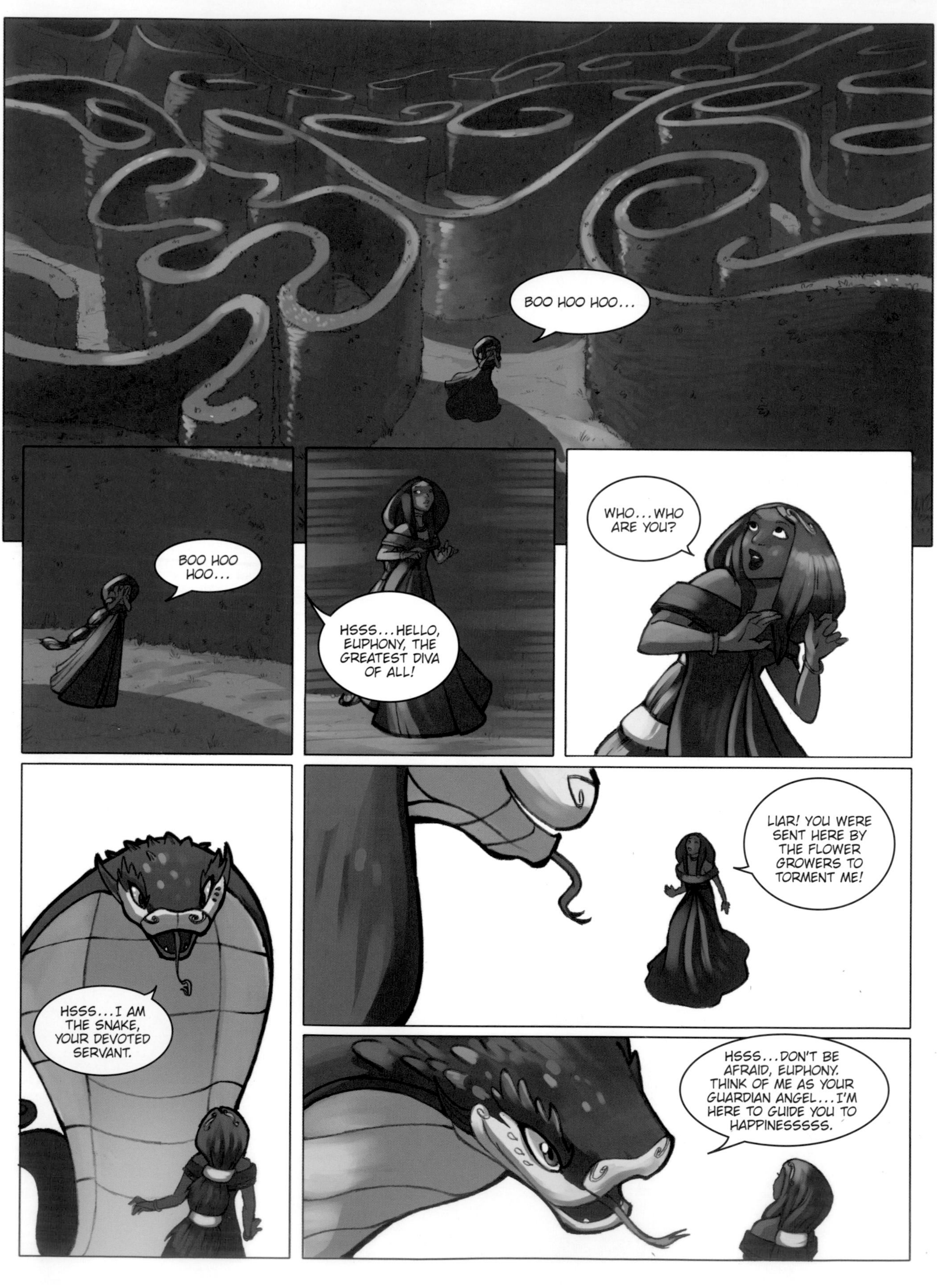
BOO HOO HOO...
BOO HOO HOO...
HSSS...HELLO, EUPHONY, THE GREATEST DIVA OF ALL!
WHO...WHO ARE YOU?
HSSS...I AM THE SNAKE, YOUR DEVOTED SERVANT.
LIAR! YOU WERE SENT HERE BY THE FLOWER GROWERS TO TORMENT ME!
HSSS...DON'T BE AFRAID, EUPHONY. THINK OF ME AS YOUR GUARDIAN ANGEL...I'M HERE TO GUIDE YOU TO HAPPINESSSSS.

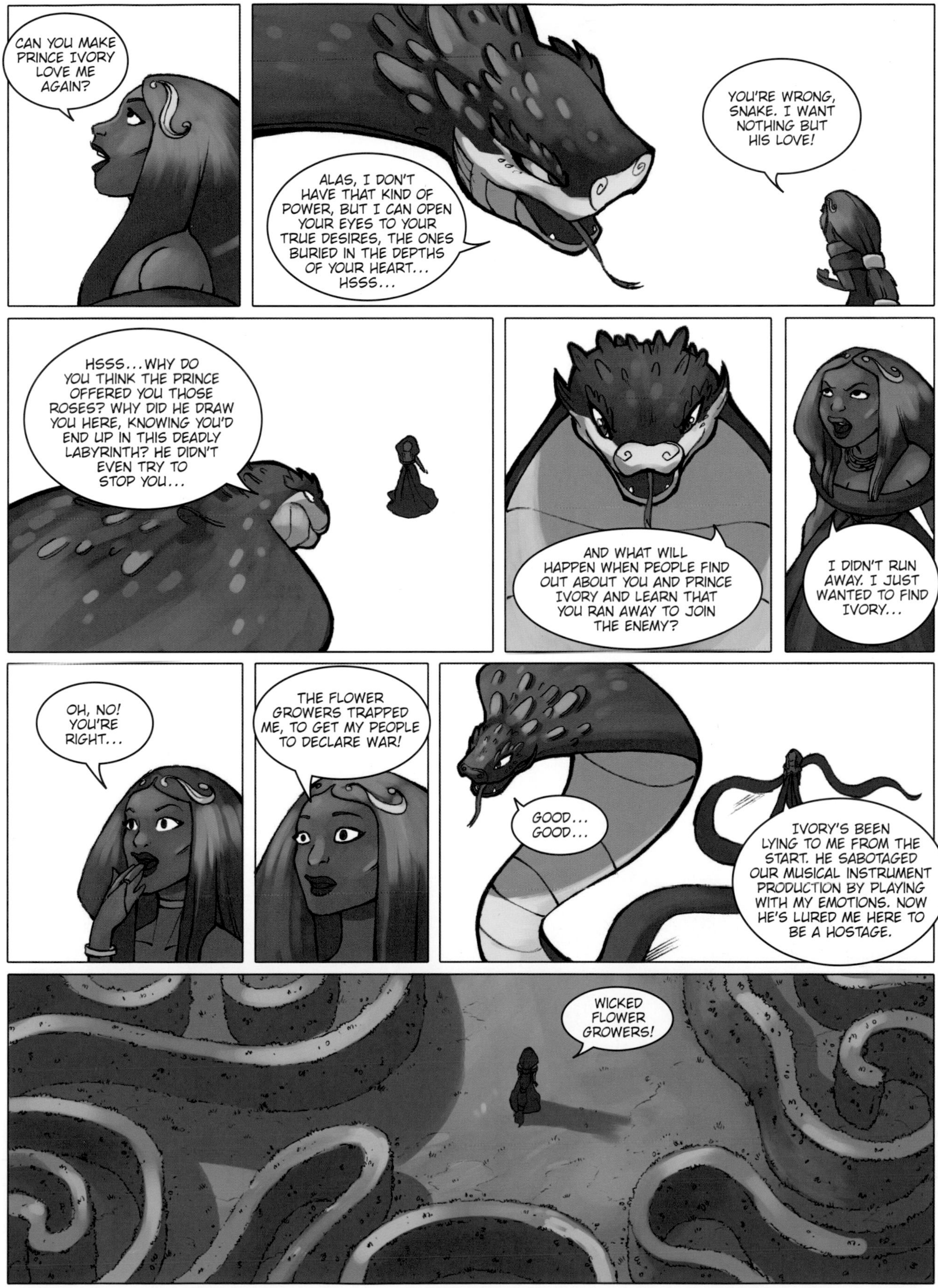
CAN YOU MAKE PRINCE IVORY LOVE ME AGAIN?
ALAS, I DON'T HAVE THAT KIND OF POWER, BUT I CAN OPEN YOUR EYES TO YOUR TRUE DESIRES, THE ONES BURIED IN THE DEPTHS OF YOUR HEART... HSSS...
YOU'RE WRONG, SNAKE. I WANT NOTHING BUT HIS LOVE!
HSSS...WHY DO YOU THINK THE PRINCE OFFERED YOU THOSE ROSES? WHY DID HE DRAW YOU HERE, KNOWING YOU'D END UP IN THIS DEADLY LABYRINTH? HE DIDN'T EVEN TRY TO STOP YOU...
AND WHAT WILL HAPPEN WHEN PEOPLE FIND OUT ABOUT YOU AND PRINCE IVORY AND LEARN THAT YOU RAN AWAY TO JOIN THE ENEMY?
I DIDN'T RUN AWAY. I JUST WANTED TO FIND IVORY...
OH, NO! YOU'RE RIGHT...
THE FLOWER GROWERS TRAPPED ME, TO GET MY PEOPLE TO DECLARE WAR!
GOOD... GOOD...
IVORY'S BEEN LYING TO ME FROM THE START. HE SABOTAGED OUR MUSICAL INSTRUMENT PRODUCTION BY PLAYING WITH MY EMOTIONS. NOW HE'S LURED ME HERE TO BE A HOSTAGE.
WICKED FLOWER GROWERS!

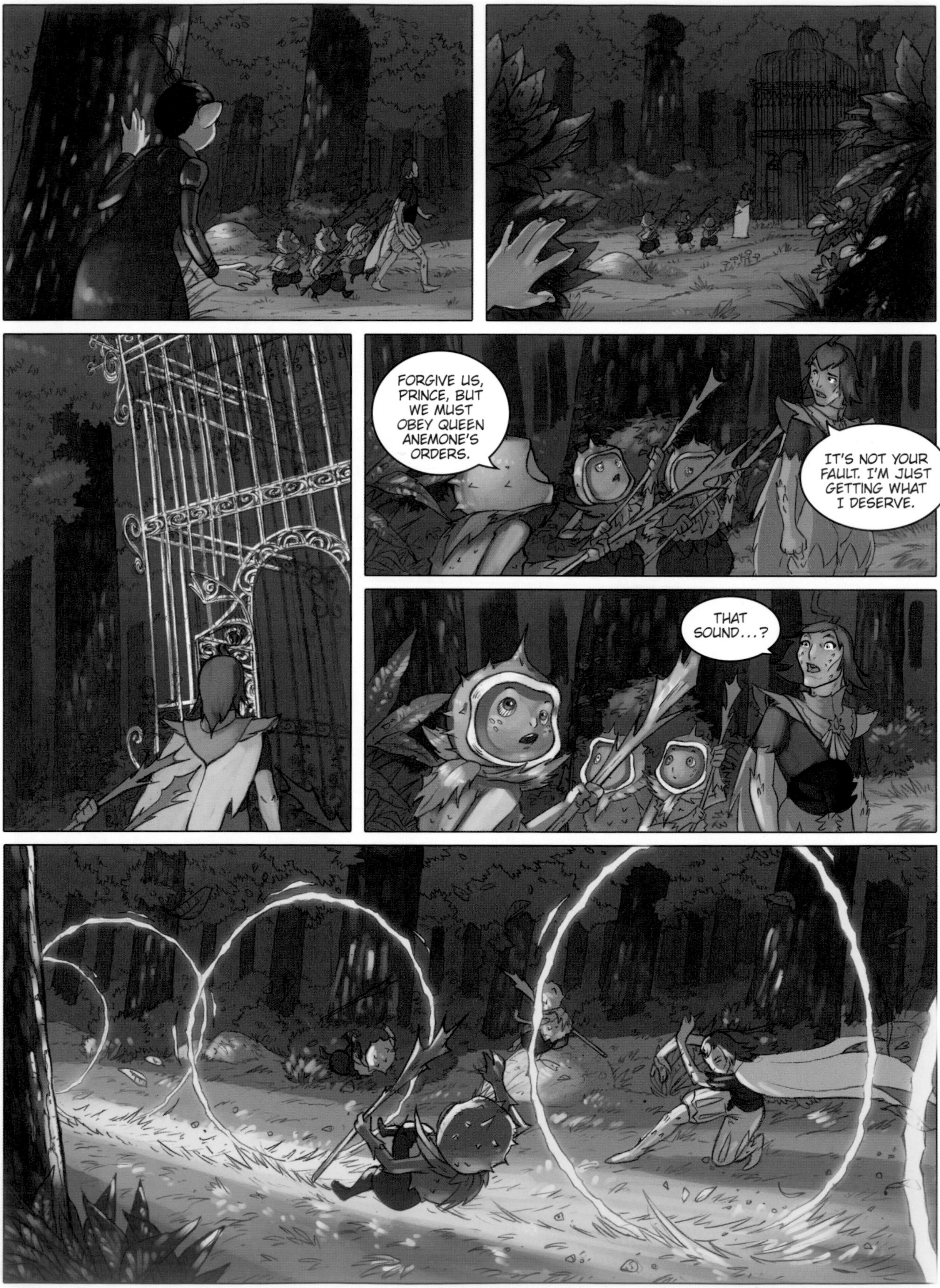
FORGIVE US, PRINCE, BUT WE MUST OBEY QUEEN ANEMONE'S ORDERS.
IT'S NOT YOUR FAULT. I'M JUST GETTING WHAT I DESERVE.
THAT SOUND...?

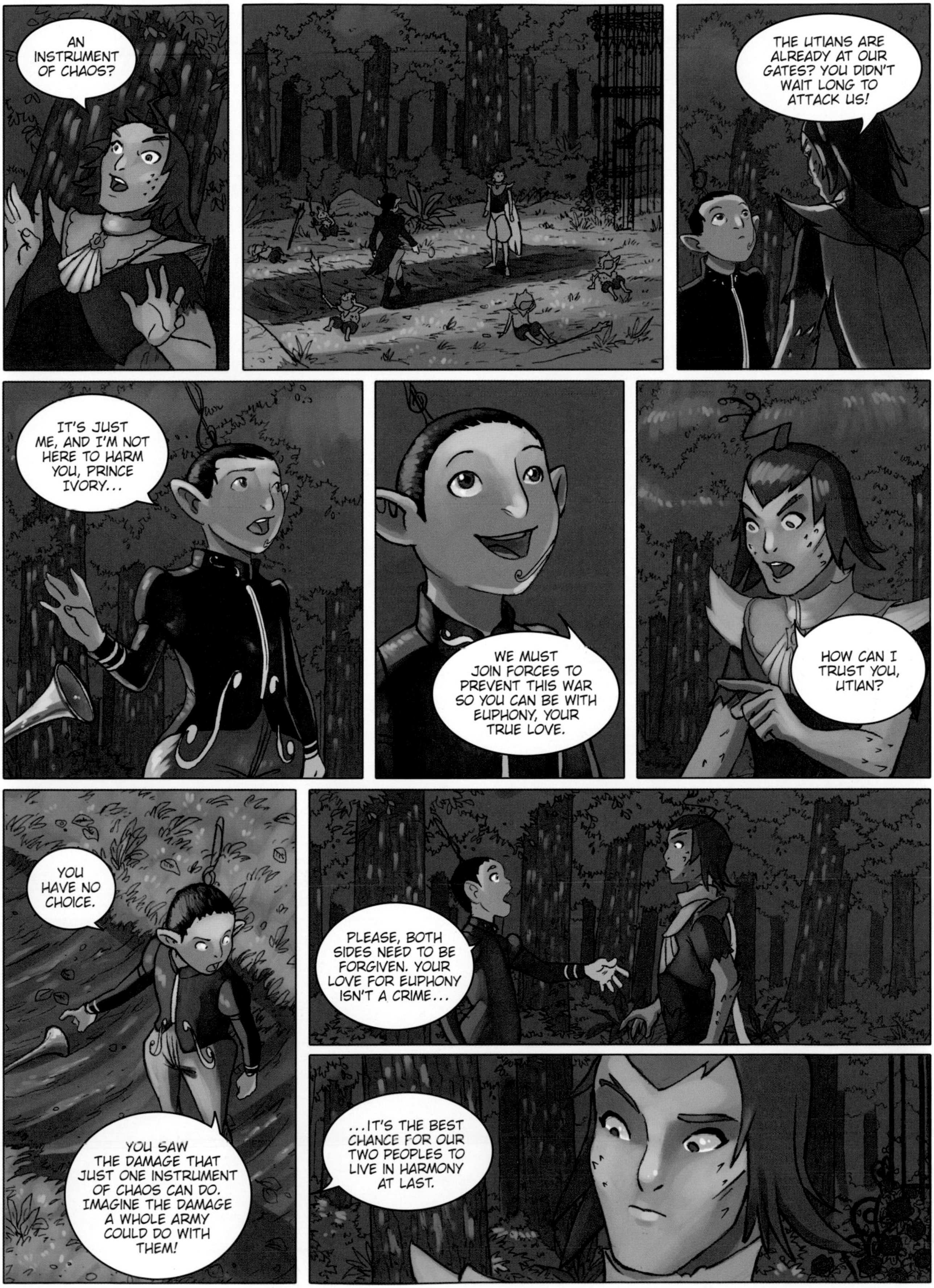
AN INSTRUMENT OF CHAOS?
THE UTIANS ARE ALREADY AT OUR GATES? YOU DIDN'T WAIT LONG TO ATTACK US!
IT'S JUST ME, AND I'M NOT HERE TO HARM YOU, PRINCE IVORY...
WE MUST JOIN FORCES TO PREVENT THIS WAR SO YOU CAN BE WITH EUPHONY, YOUR TRUE LOVE.
HOW CAN I TRUST YOU, UTIAN?
YOU HAVE NO CHOICE.
YOU SAW THE DAMAGE THAT JUST ONE INSTRUMENT OF CHAOS CAN DO. IMAGINE THE DAMAGE A WHOLE ARMY COULD DO WITH THEM!
PLEASE, BOTH SIDES NEED TO BE FORGIVEN. YOUR LOVE FOR EUPHONY ISN'T A CRIME...
...IT'S THE BEST CHANCE FOR OUR TWO PEOPLES TO LIVE IN HARMONY AT LAST.

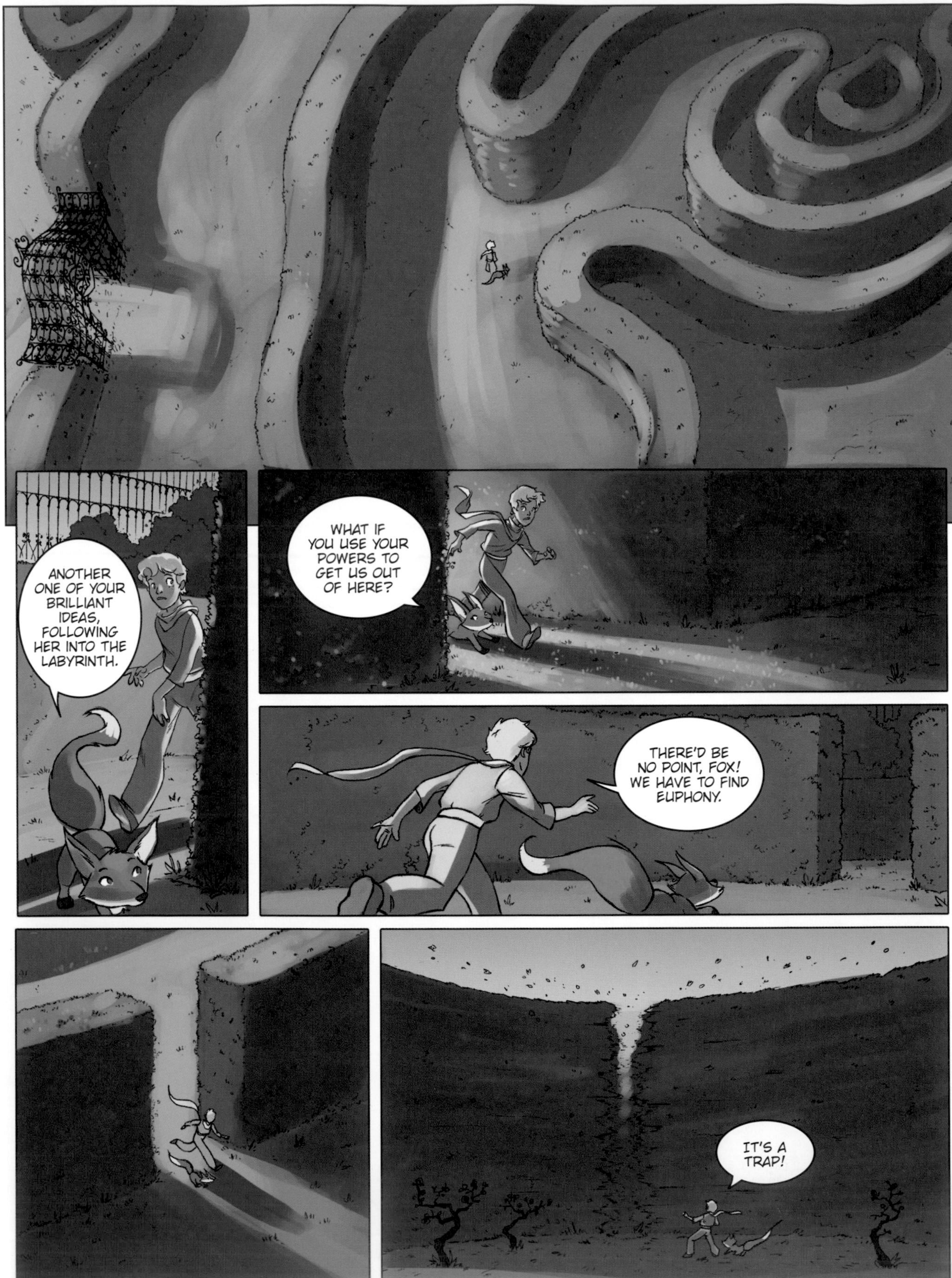
ANOTHER ONE OF YOUR BRILLIANT IDEAS, FOLLOWING HER INTO THE LABYRINTH.
WHAT IF YOU USE YOUR POWERS TO GET US OUT OF HERE?
THERE'D BE NO POINT, FOX! WE HAVE TO FIND EUPHONY.
IT'S A TRAP!

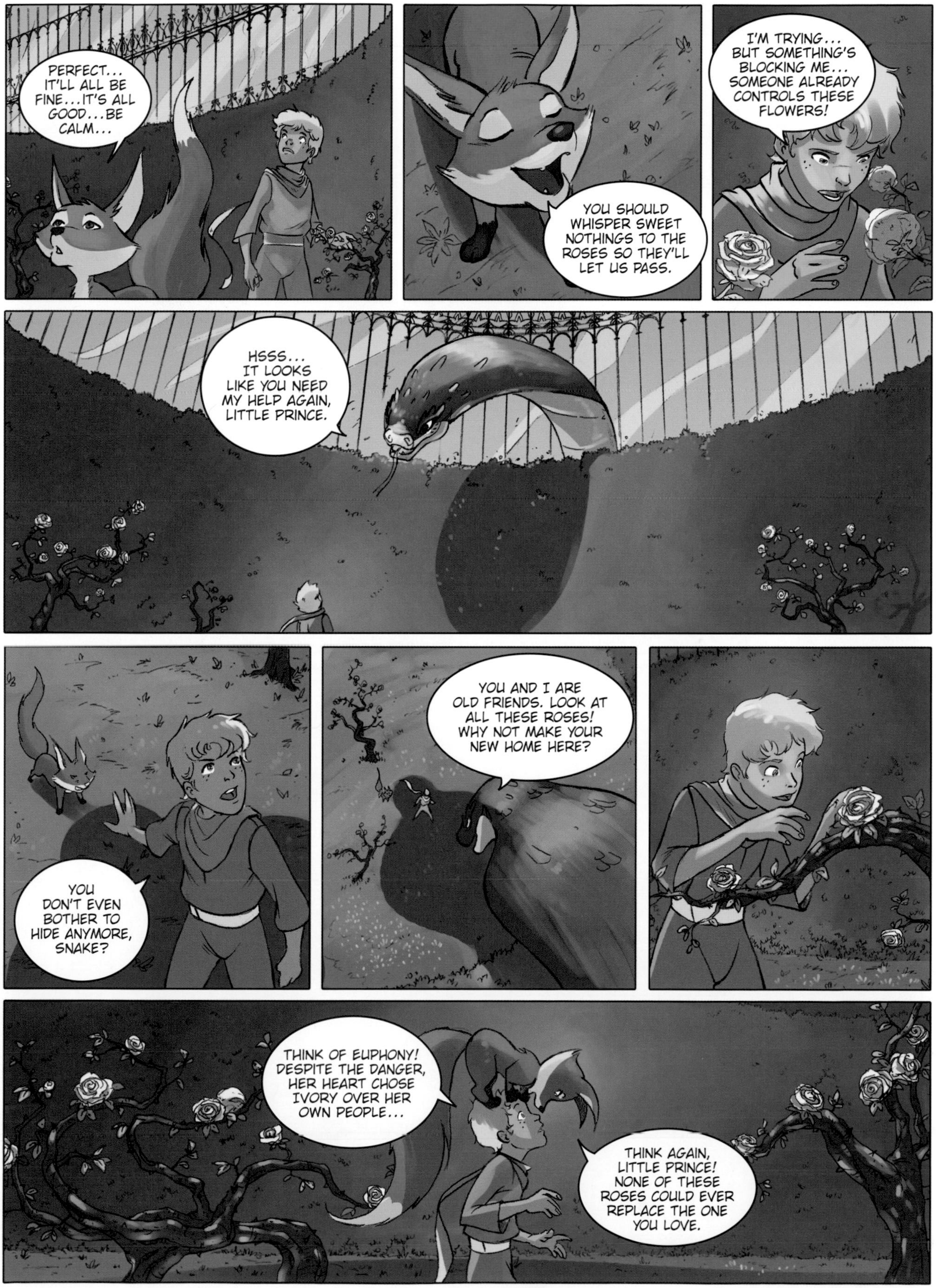
PERFECT... IT'LL ALL BE FINE...IT'S ALL GOOD...BE CALM...
YOU SHOULD WHISPER SWEET NOTHINGS TO THE ROSES SO THEY'LL LET US PASS.
I'M TRYING... BUT SOMETHING'S BLOCKING ME... SOMEONE ALREADY CONTROLS THESE FLOWERS!
HSSS... IT LOOKS LIKE YOU NEED MY HELP AGAIN, LITTLE PRINCE.
YOU DON'T EVEN BOTHER TO HIDE ANYMORE, SNAKE?
YOU AND I ARE OLD FRIENDS. LOOK AT ALL THESE ROSES! WHY NOT MAKE YOUR NEW HOME HERE?
THINK OF EUPHONY! DESPITE THE DANGER, HER HEART CHOSE IVORY OVER HER OWN PEOPLE...
THINK AGAIN, LITTLE PRINCE! NONE OF THESE ROSES COULD EVER REPLACE THE ONE YOU LOVE.

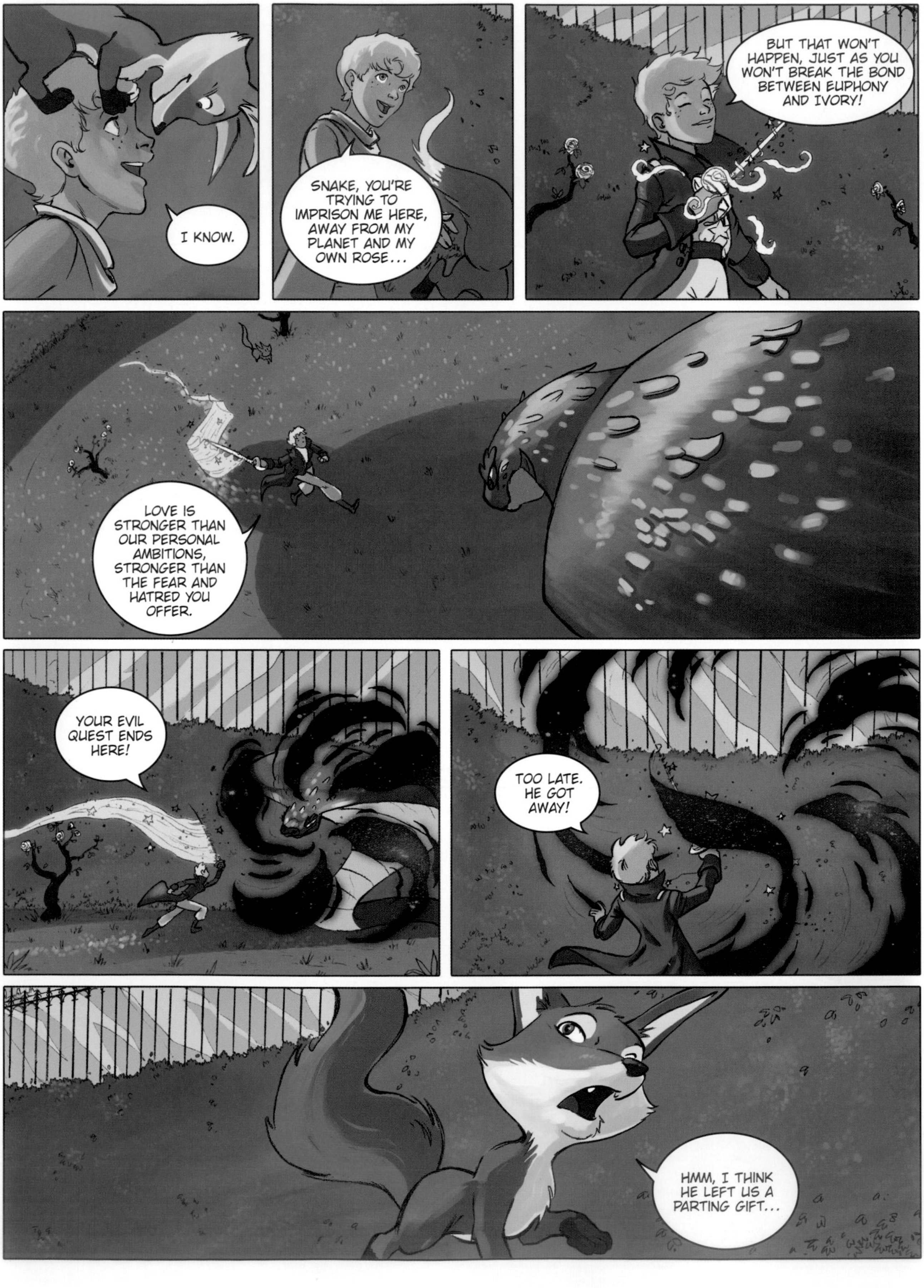
I KNOW.
SNAKE, YOU'RE TRYING TO IMPRISON ME HERE, AWAY FROM MY PLANET AND MY OWN ROSE...
BUT THAT WON'T HAPPEN, JUST AS YOU WON'T BREAK THE BOND BETWEEN EUPHONY AND IVORY!
LOVE IS STRONGER THAN OUR PERSONAL AMBITIONS, STRONGER THAN THE FEAR AND HATRED YOU OFFER.
YOUR EVIL QUEST ENDS HERE!
TOO LATE. HE GOT AWAY!
HMM, I THINK HE LEFT US A PARTING GIFT...

THE GLOOMIES! AND WE CAN'T ESCAPE!

HA! DON'T TELL ME THE UNFLAPPABLE FOX IS AFRAID!

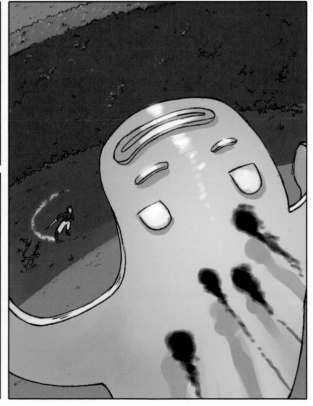

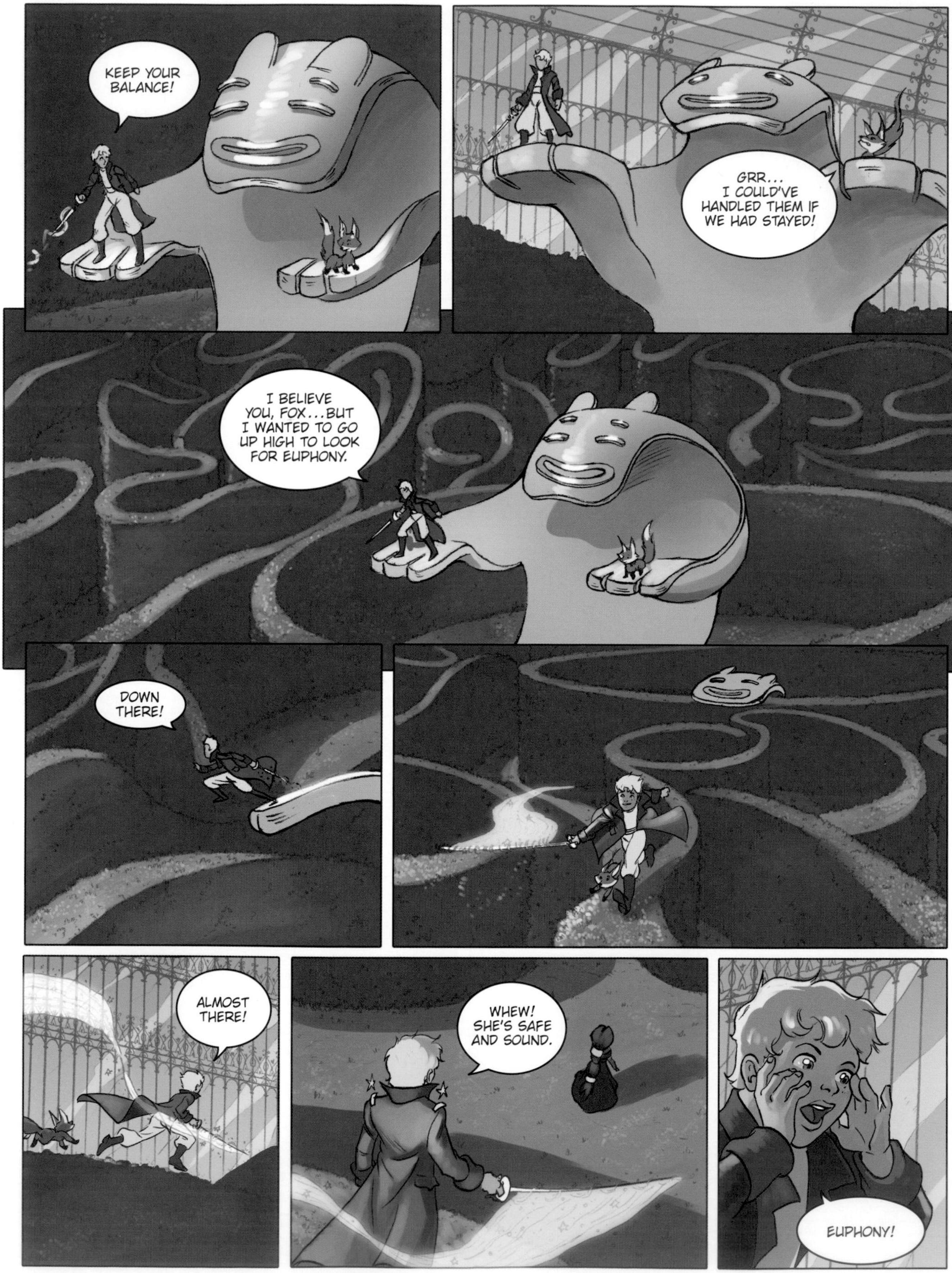
KEEP YOUR BALANCE!
GRR... I COULD'VE HANDLED THEM IF WE HAD STAYED!
I BELIEVE YOU, FOX...BUT I WANTED TO GO UP HIGH TO LOOK FOR EUPHONY.
DOWN THERE!
ALMOST THERE!
WHEW! SHE'S SAFE AND SOUND.
EUPHONY!

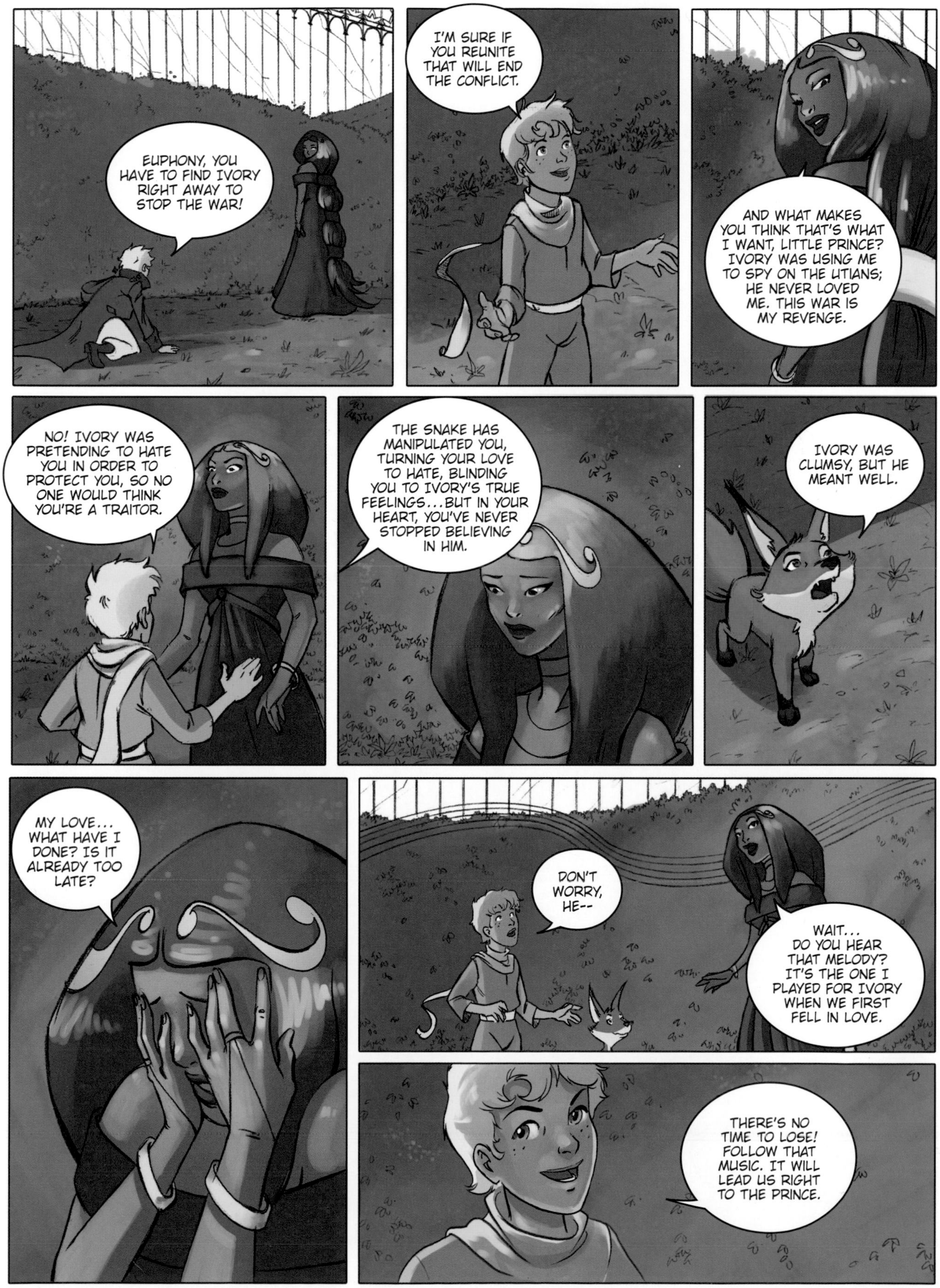
EUPHONY, YOU HAVE TO FIND IVORY RIGHT AWAY TO STOP THE WAR!
I'M SURE IF YOU REUNITE THAT WILL END THE CONFLICT.
AND WHAT MAKES YOU THINK THAT'S WHAT I WANT, LITTLE PRINCE? IVORY WAS USING ME TO SPY ON THE UTIANS; HE NEVER LOVED ME. THIS WAR IS MY REVENGE.
NO! IVORY WAS PRETENDING TO HATE YOU IN ORDER TO PROTECT YOU, SO NO ONE WOULD THINK YOU'RE A TRAITOR.
THE SNAKE HAS MANIPULATED YOU, TURNING YOUR LOVE TO HATE, BLINDING YOU TO IVORY'S TRUE FEELINGS...BUT IN YOUR HEART, YOU'VE NEVER STOPPED BELIEVING IN HIM.
IVORY WAS CLUMSY, BUT HE MEANT WELL.
MY LOVE... WHAT HAVE I DONE? IS IT ALREADY TOO LATE?
DON'T WORRY, HE--
WAIT... DO YOU HEAR THAT MELODY? IT'S THE ONE I PLAYED FOR IVORY WHEN WE FIRST FELL IN LOVE.
THERE'S NO TIME TO LOSE! FOLLOW THAT MUSIC. IT WILL LEAD US RIGHT TO THE PRINCE.

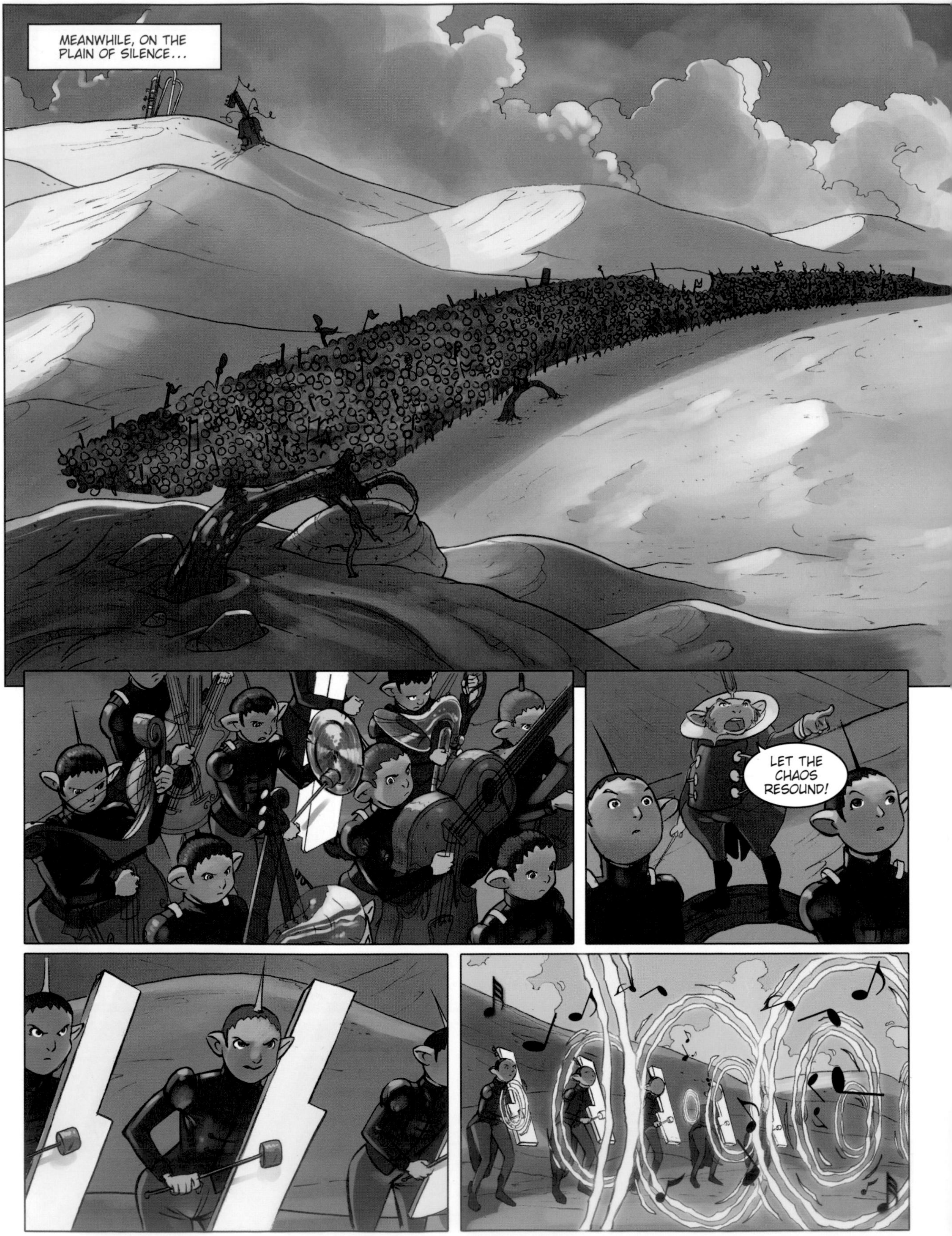
MEANWHILE, ON THE PLAIN OF SILENCE...
LET THE CHAOS RESOUND!

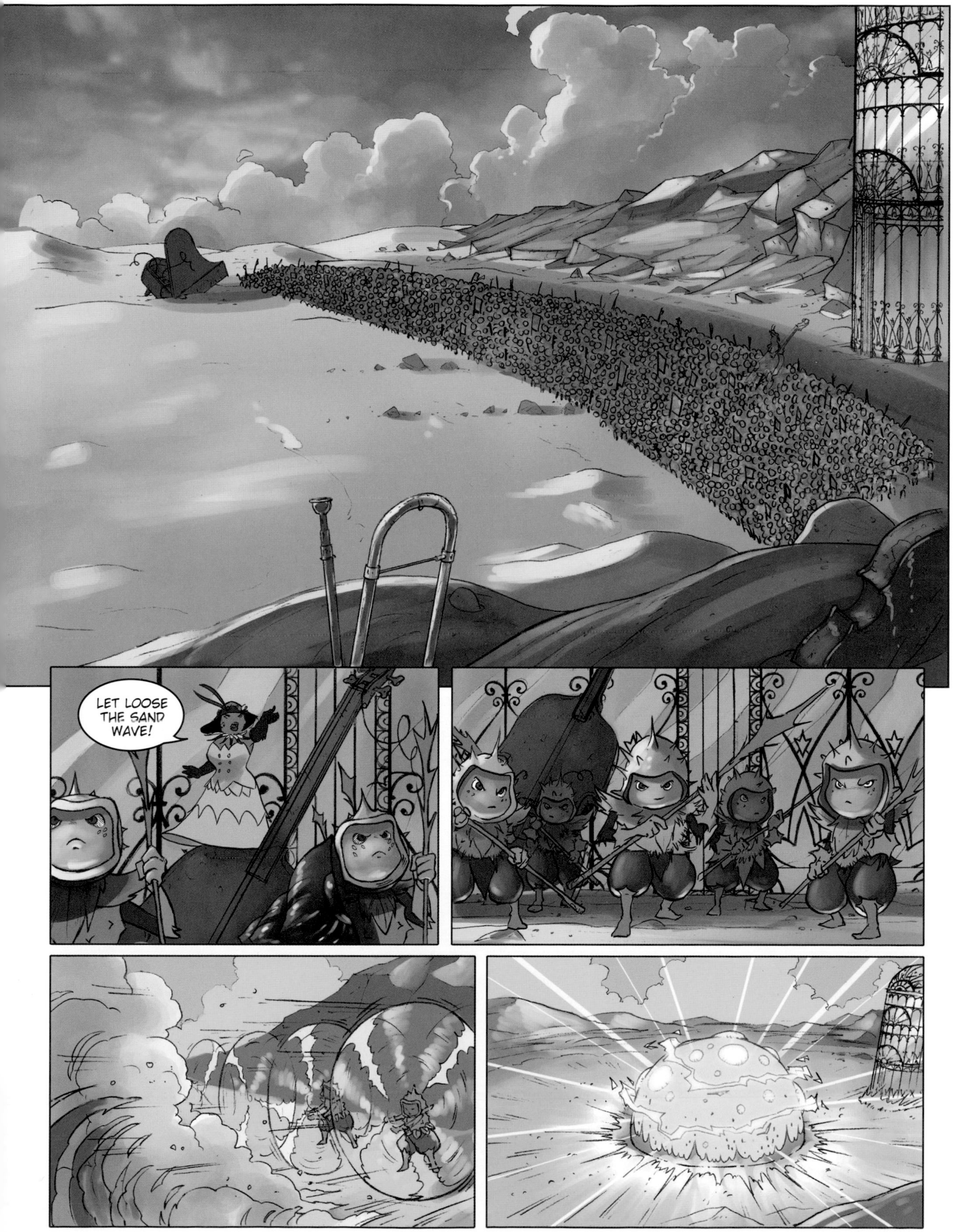
LET LOOSE THE SAND WAVE!

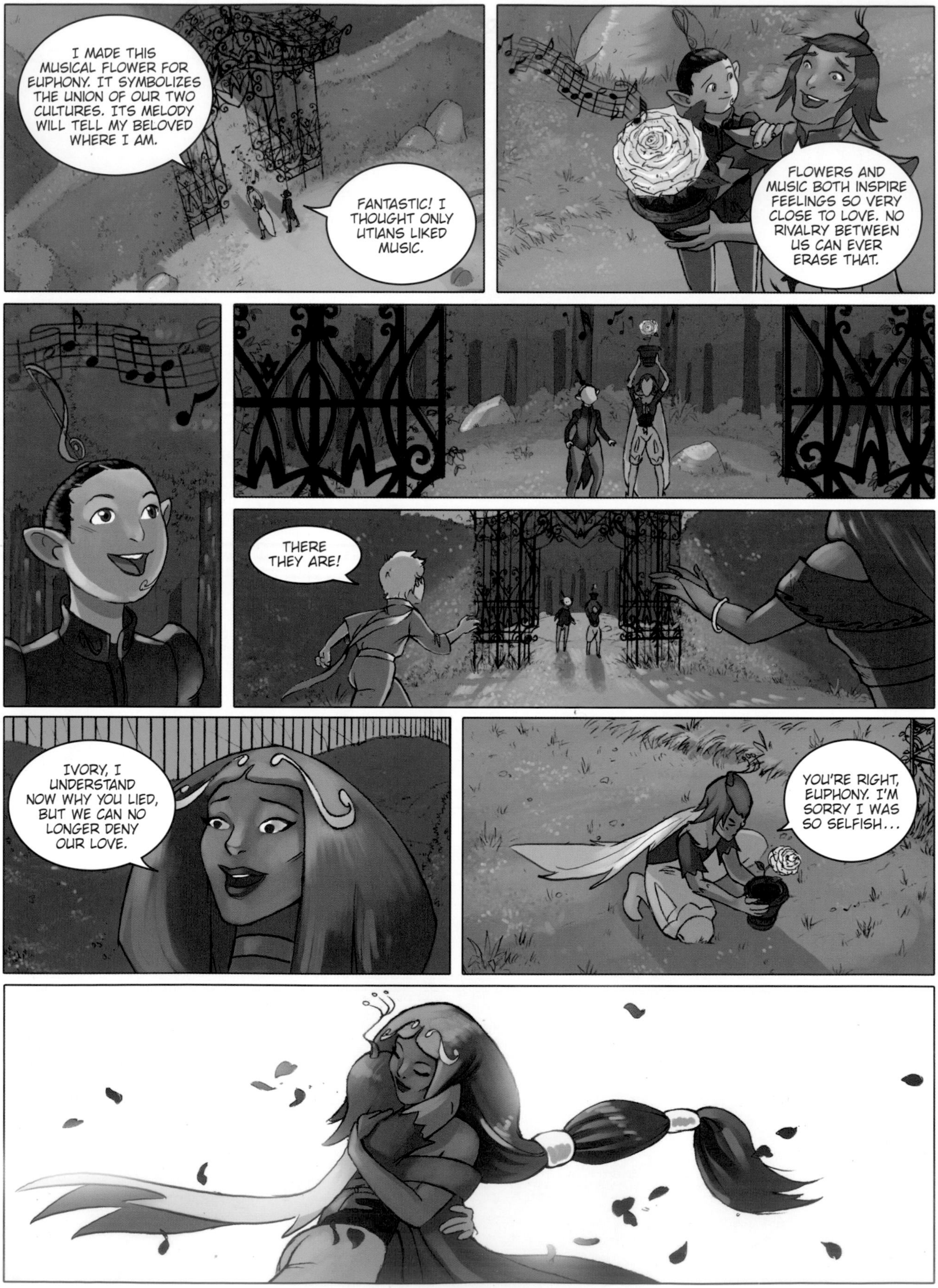
I MADE THIS MUSICAL FLOWER FOR EUPHONY. IT SYMBOLIZES THE UNION OF OUR TWO CULTURES. ITS MELODY WILL TELL MY BELOVED WHERE I AM.
FANTASTIC! I THOUGHT ONLY UTIANS LIKED MUSIC.
FLOWERS AND MUSIC BOTH INSPIRE FEELINGS SO VERY CLOSE TO LOVE. NO RIVALRY BETWEEN US CAN EVER ERASE THAT.
THERE THEY ARE!
IVORY, I UNDERSTAND NOW WHY YOU LIED, BUT WE CAN NO LONGER DENY OUR LOVE.
YOU'RE RIGHT, EUPHONY. I'M SORRY I WAS SO SELFISH...

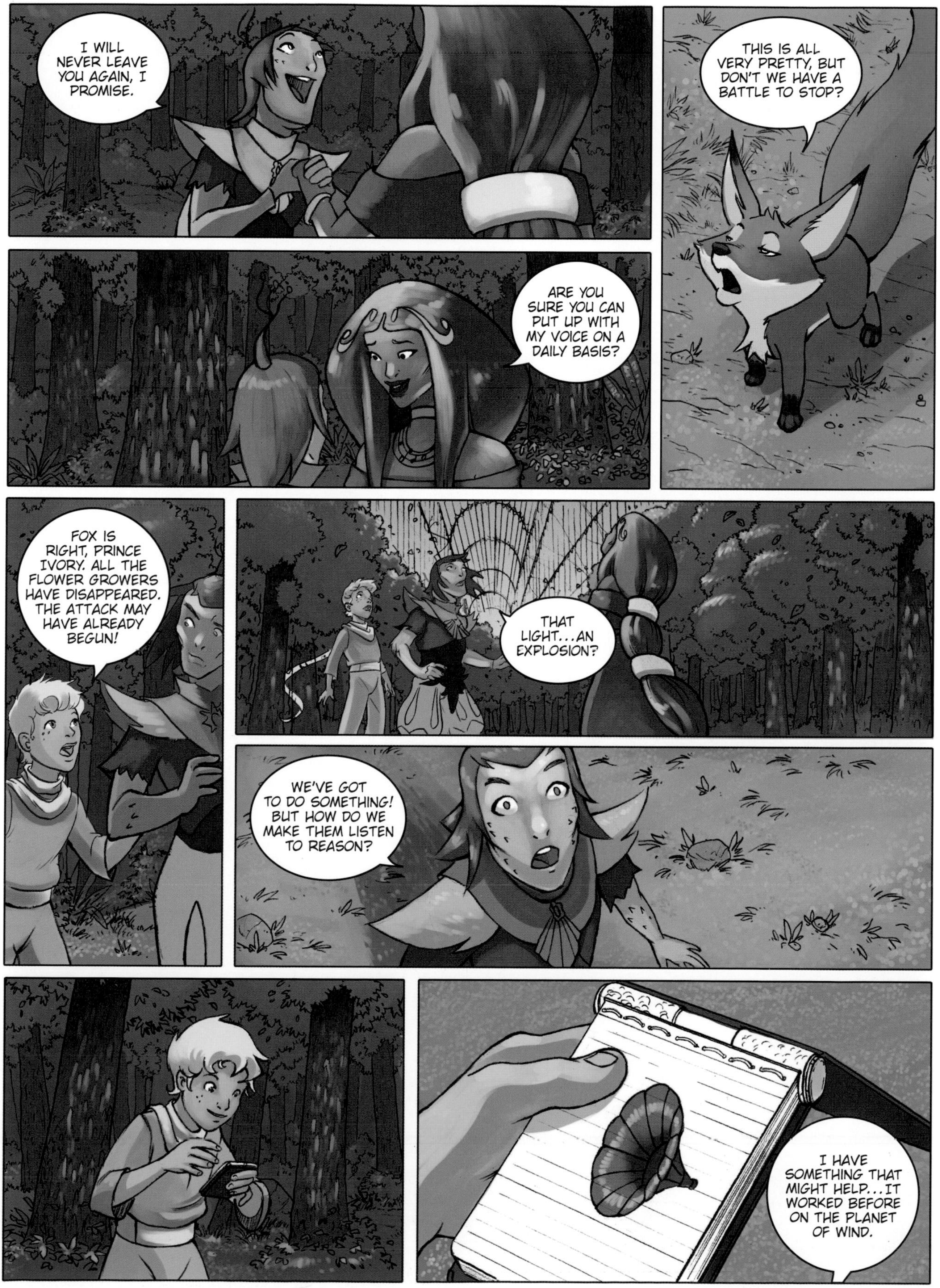

I WILL NEVER LEAVE YOU AGAIN, I PROMISE.
ARE YOU SURE YOU CAN PUT UP WITH MY VOICE ON A DAILY BASIS?
THIS IS ALL VERY PRETTY, BUT DON'T WE HAVE A BATTLE TO STOP?
FOX IS RIGHT, PRINCE IVORY. ALL THE FLOWER GROWERS HAVE DISAPPEARED. THE ATTACK MAY HAVE ALREADY BEGUN!
THAT LIGHT...AN EXPLOSION?
WE'VE GOT TO DO SOMETHING! BUT HOW DO WE MAKE THEM LISTEN TO REASON?
I HAVE SOMETHING THAT MIGHT HELP...IT WORKED BEFORE ON THE PLANET OF WIND.

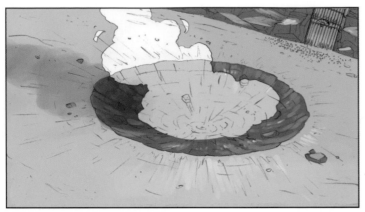

WE NEED TO GET CLOSER. THE UTIANS CAN JUST STAY BACK AND PLAY THEIR CHAOS INSTRUMENTS WHILE WE WEAR OURSELVES OUT MAKING SAND WAVES!

CHARGE!

THE FOOLS HAVE FALLEN INTO MY TRAP!

USE THE BASSES! SMASH THEM!

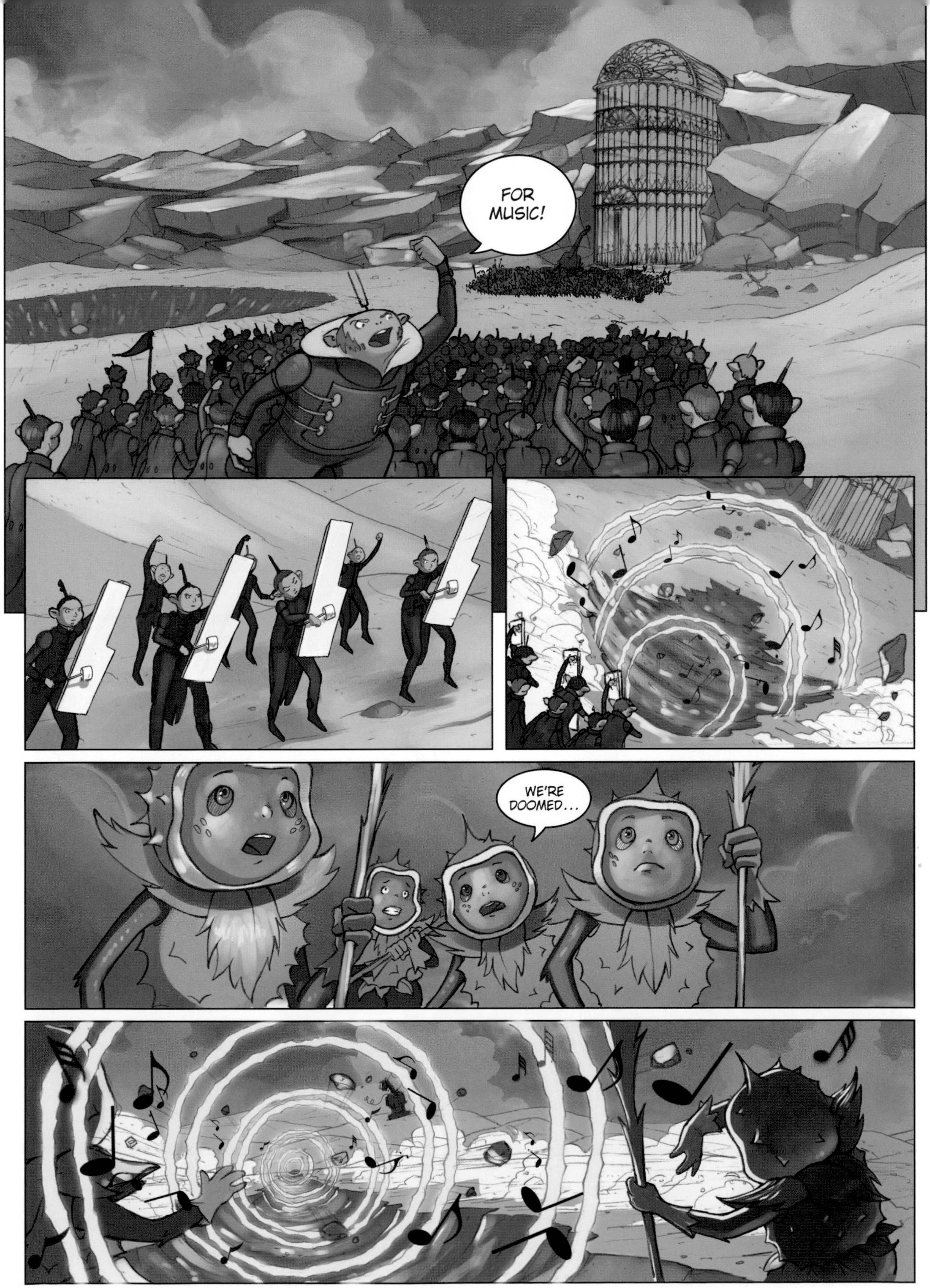
FOR MUSIC!
WE'RE DOOMED...

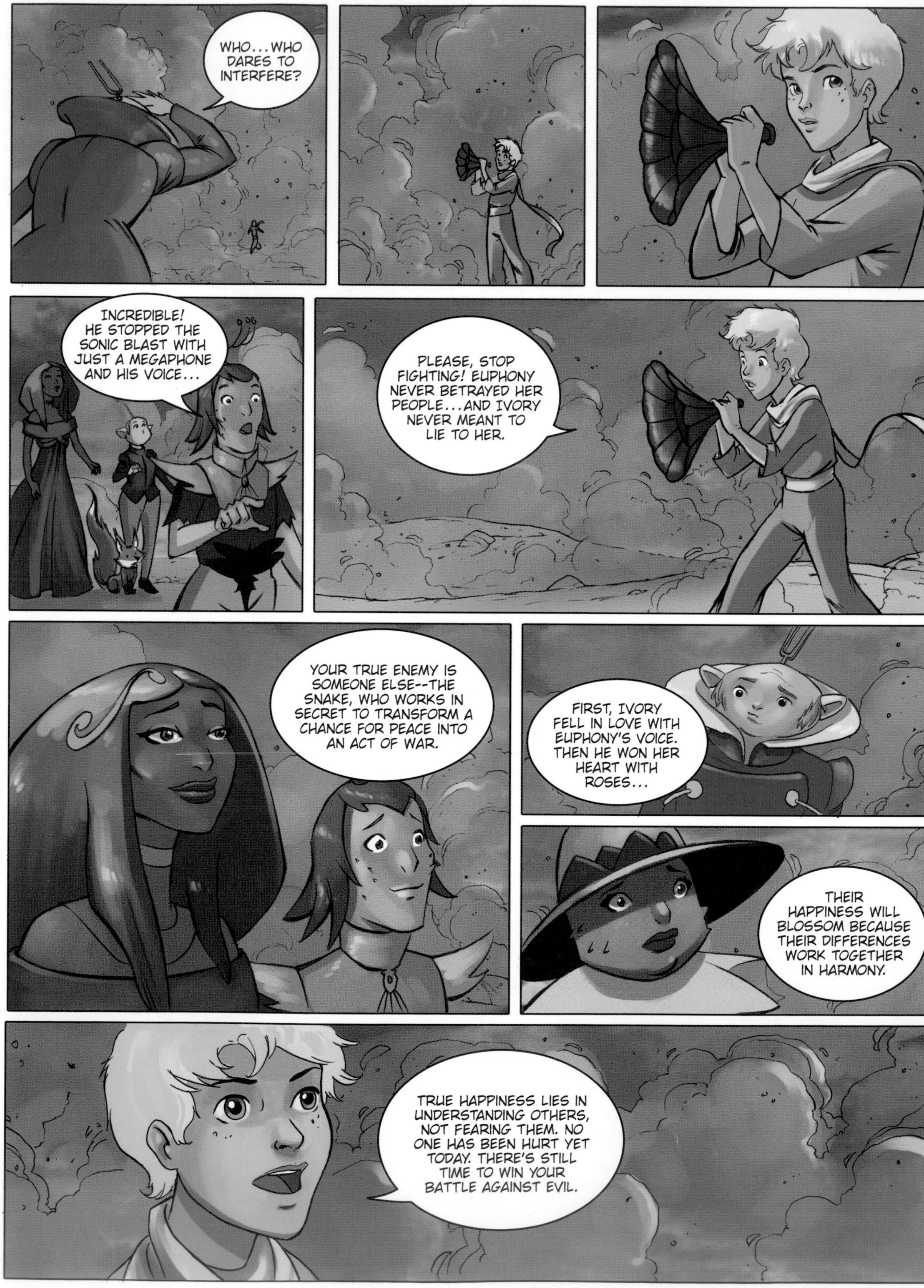
WHO...WHO DARES TO INTERFERE?
INCREDIBLE! HE STOPPED THE SONIC BLAST WITH JUST A MEGAPHONE AND HIS VOICE...
PLEASE, STOP FIGHTING! EUPHONY NEVER BETRAYED HER PEOPLE...AND IVORY NEVER MEANT TO LIE TO HER.
YOUR TRUE ENEMY IS SOMEONE ELSE--THE SNAKE, WHO WORKS IN SECRET TO TRANSFORM A CHANCE FOR PEACE INTO AN ACT OF WAR.
FIRST, IVORY FELL IN LOVE WITH EUPHONY'S VOICE. THEN HE WON HER HEART WITH ROSES...
THEIR HAPPINESS WILL BLOSSOM BECAUSE THEIR DIFFERENCES WORK TOGETHER IN HARMONY.
TRUE HAPPINESS LIES IN UNDERSTANDING OTHERS, NOT FEARING THEM. NO ONE HAS BEEN HURT YET TODAY. THERE'S STILL TIME TO WIN YOUR BATTLE AGAINST EVIL.

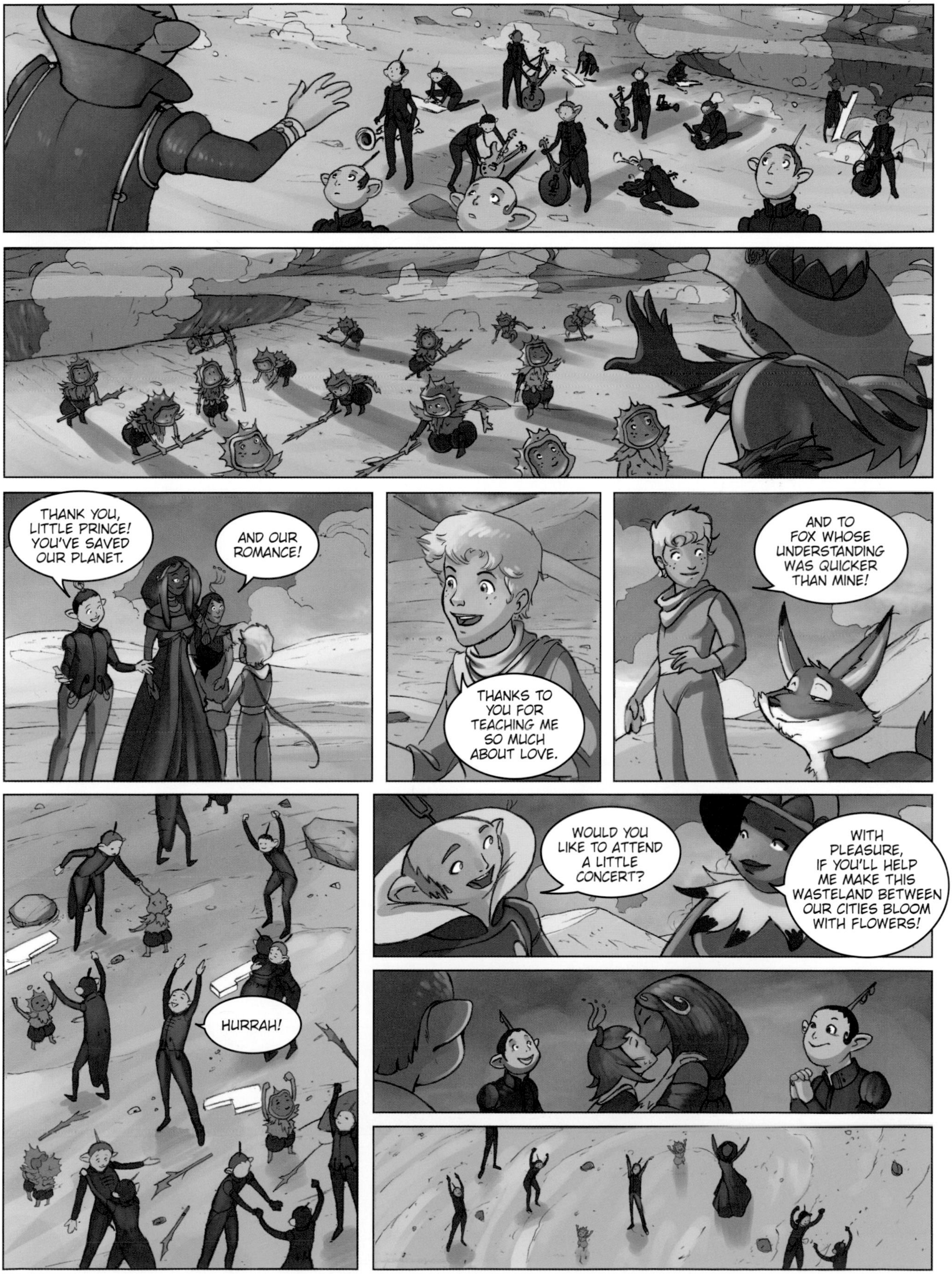
THANK YOU, LITTLE PRINCE! YOU'VE SAVED OUR PLANET.
AND OUR ROMANCE!
THANKS TO YOU FOR TEACHING ME SO MUCH ABOUT LOVE.
AND TO FOX WHOSE UNDERSTANDING WAS QUICKER THAN MINE!
HURRAH!
WOULD YOU LIKE TO ATTEND A LITTLE CONCERT?
WITH PLEASURE, IF YOU'LL HELP ME MAKE THIS WASTELAND BETWEEN OUR CITIES BLOOM WITH FLOWERS!

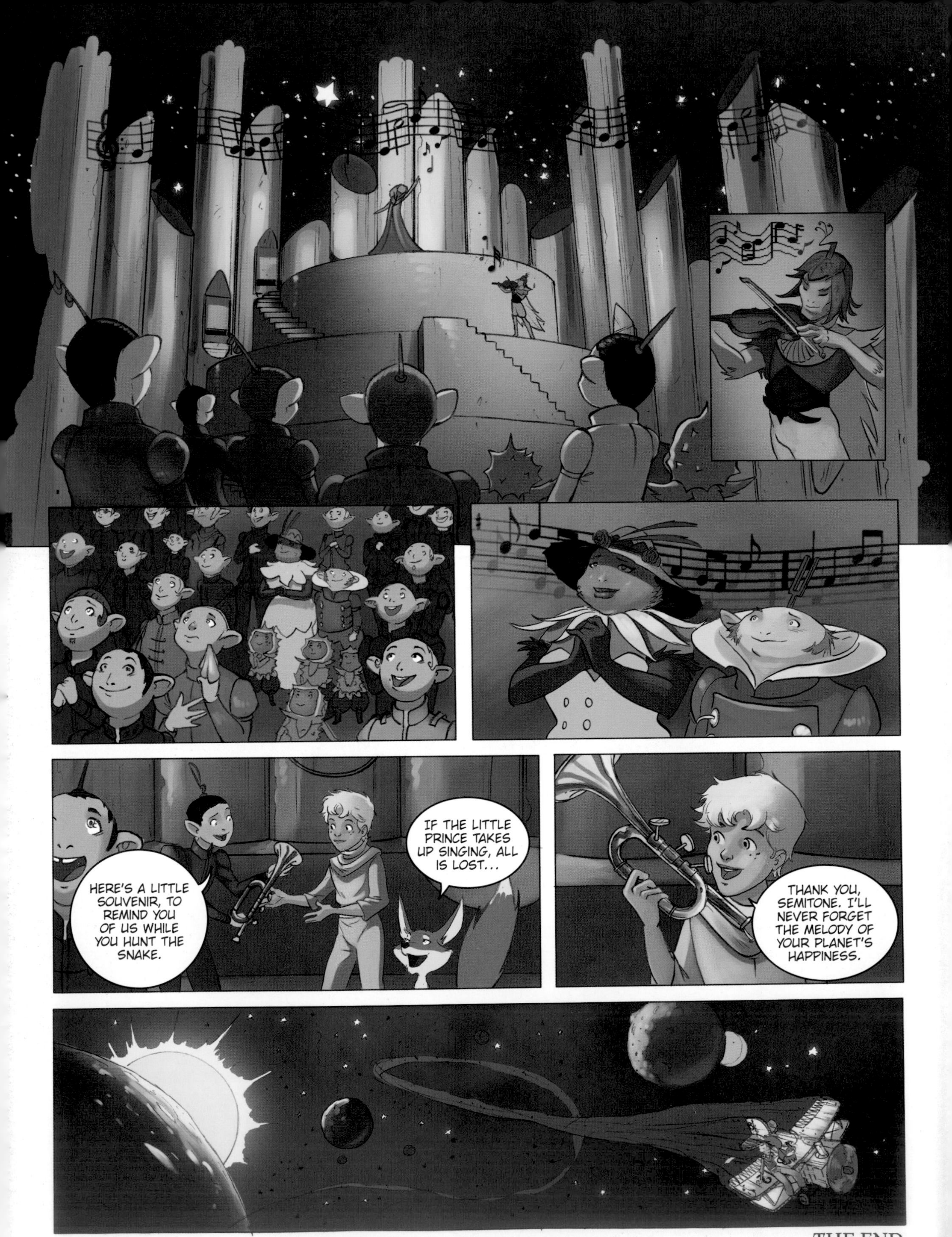
HERE'S A LITTLE SOUVENIR, TO REMIND YOU OF US WHILE YOU HUNT THE SNAKE.
IF THE LITTLE PRINCE TAKES UP SINGING, ALL IS LOST...
THANK YOU, SEMITONE. I'LL NEVER FORGET THE MELODY OF YOUR PLANET'S HAPPINESS.

THE END

The Little Prince

AS IMAGINED BY

CONVARD

&

GRIFFO

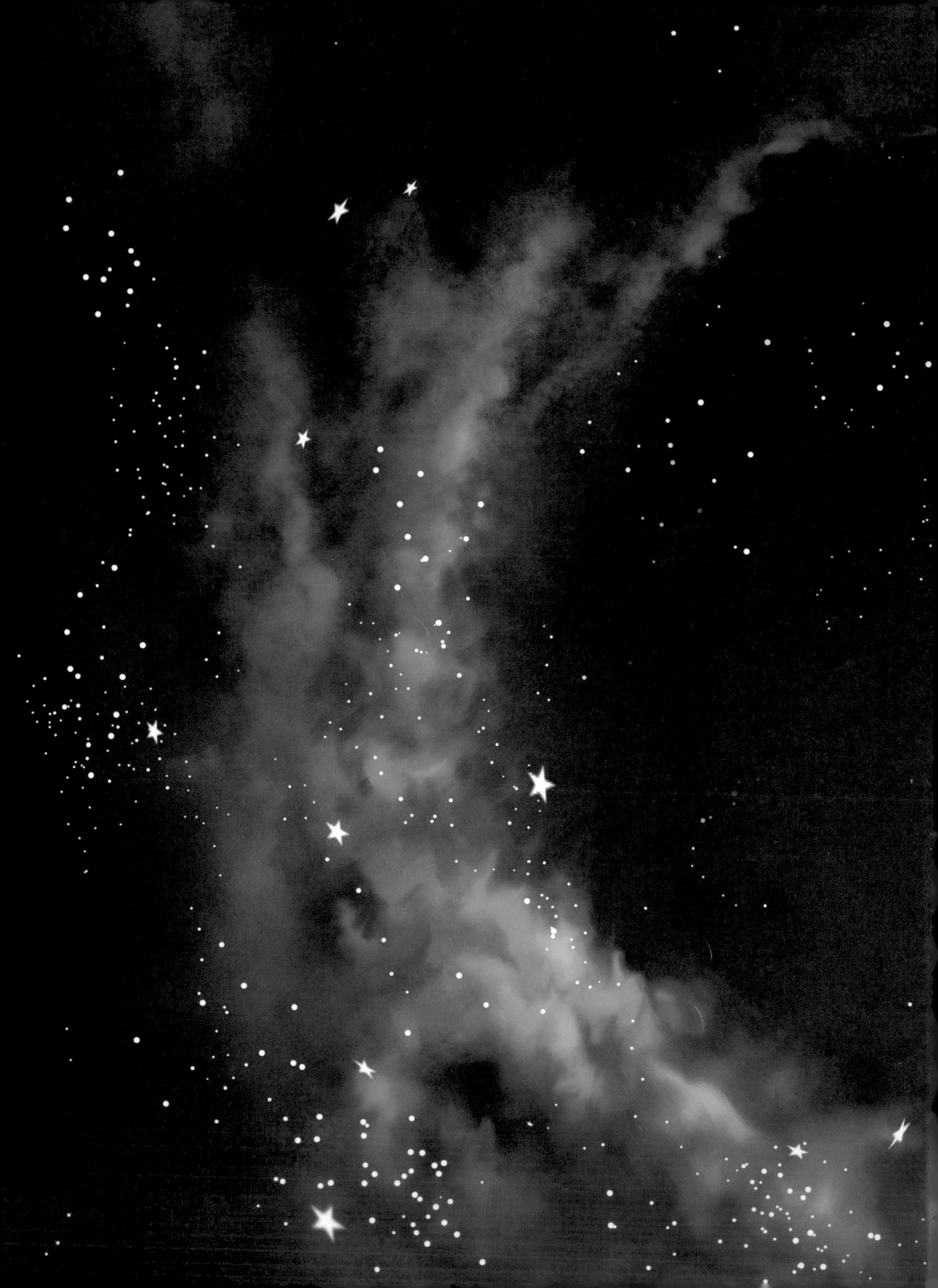

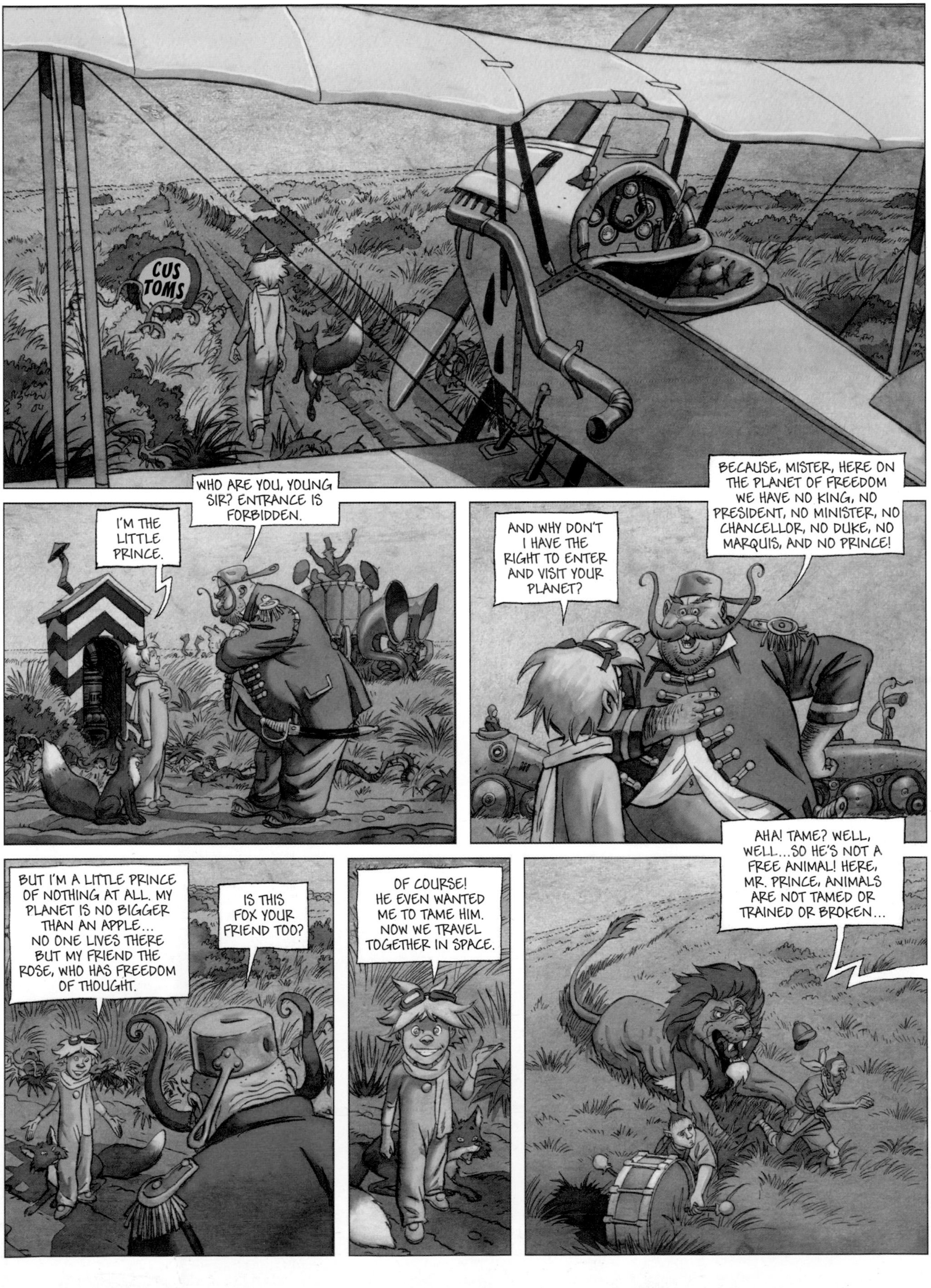
CUS TOMS
WHO ARE YOU, YOUNG SIR? ENTRANCE IS FORBIDDEN.
I'M THE LITTLE PRINCE.
AND WHY DON'T I HAVE THE RIGHT TO ENTER AND VISIT YOUR PLANET?
BECAUSE, MISTER, HERE ON THE PLANET OF FREEDOM WE HAVE NO KING, NO PRESIDENT, NO MINISTER, NO CHANCELLOR, NO DUKE, NO MARQUIS, AND NO PRINCE!
BUT I'M A LITTLE PRINCE OF NOTHING AT ALL. MY PLANET IS NO BIGGER THAN AN APPLE... NO ONE LIVES THERE BUT MY FRIEND THE ROSE, WHO HAS FREEDOM OF THOUGHT.
IS THIS FOX YOUR FRIEND TOO?
OF COURSE! HE EVEN WANTED ME TO TAME HIM. NOW WE TRAVEL TOGETHER IN SPACE.
AHA! TAME? WELL, WELL...SO HE'S NOT A FREE ANIMAL! HERE, MR. PRINCE, ANIMALS ARE NOT TAMED OR TRAINED OR BROKEN...

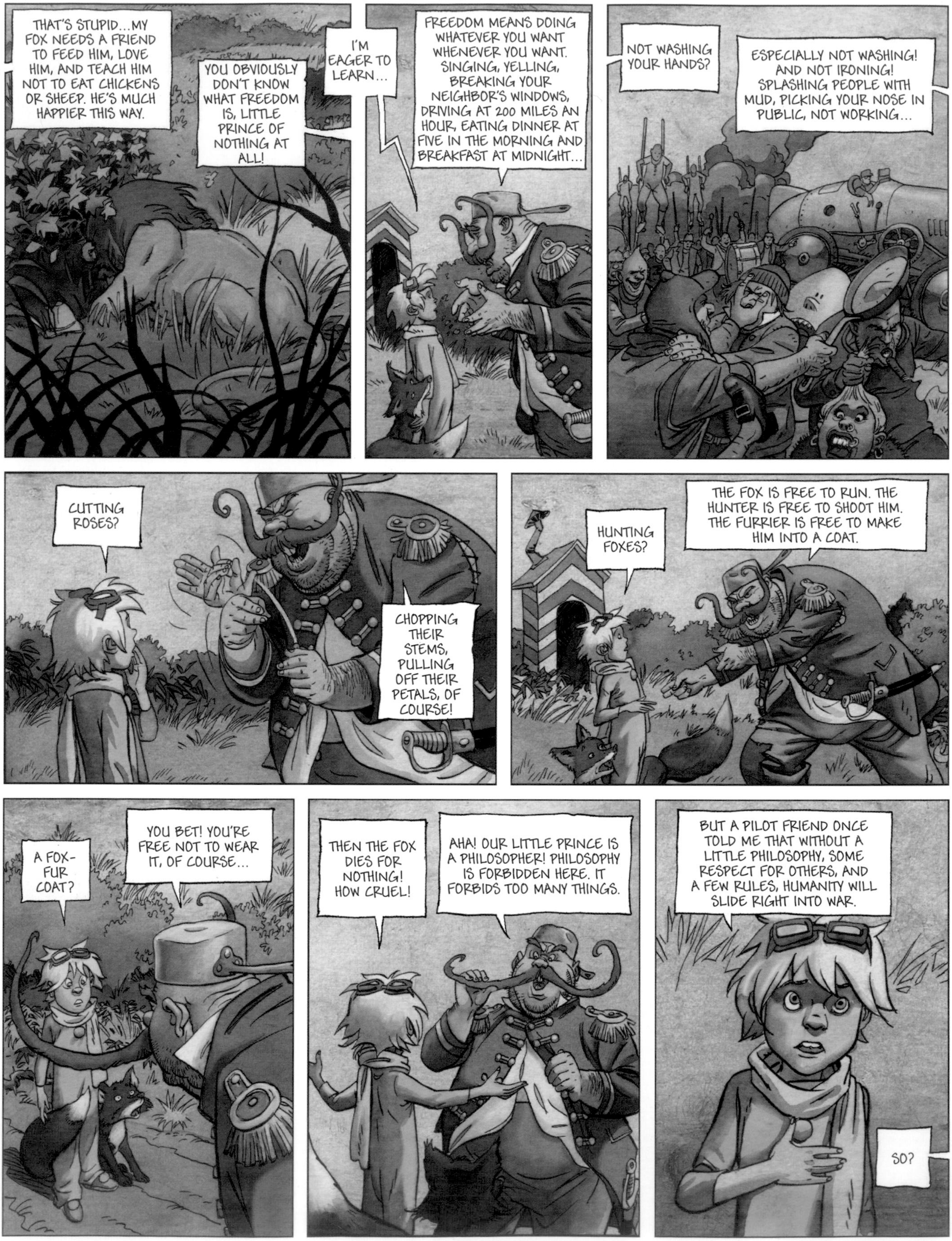
THAT'S STUPID...MY FOX NEEDS A FRIEND TO FEED HIM, LOVE HIM, AND TEACH HIM NOT TO EAT CHICKENS OR SHEEP. HE'S MUCH HAPPIER THIS WAY.
YOU OBVIOUSLY DON'T KNOW WHAT FREEDOM IS, LITTLE PRINCE OF NOTHING AT ALL!
I'M EAGER TO LEARN...
FREEDOM MEANS DOING WHATEVER YOU WANT WHENEVER YOU WANT. SINGING, YELLING, BREAKING YOUR NEIGHBOR'S WINDOWS, DRIVING AT 200 MILES AN HOUR, EATING DINNER AT FIVE IN THE MORNING AND BREAKFAST AT MIDNIGHT...
NOT WASHING YOUR HANDS?
ESPECIALLY NOT WASHING! AND NOT IRONING! SPLASHING PEOPLE WITH MUD, PICKING YOUR NOSE IN PUBLIC, NOT WORKING...
CUTTING ROSES?
CHOPPING THEIR STEMS, PULLING OFF THEIR PETALS, OF COURSE!
HUNTING FOXES?
THE FOX IS FREE TO RUN. THE HUNTER IS FREE TO SHOOT HIM. THE FURRIER IS FREE TO MAKE HIM INTO A COAT.
A FOX-FUR COAT?
YOU BET! YOU'RE FREE NOT TO WEAR IT, OF COURSE...
THEN THE FOX DIES FOR NOTHING! HOW CRUEL!
AHA! OUR LITTLE PRINCE IS A PHILOSOPHER! PHILOSOPHY IS FORBIDDEN HERE. IT FORBIDS TOO MANY THINGS.
BUT A PILOT FRIEND ONCE TOLD ME THAT WITHOUT A LITTLE PHILOSOPHY, SOME RESPECT FOR OTHERS, AND A FEW RULES, HUMANITY WILL SLIDE RIGHT INTO WAR.
SO?

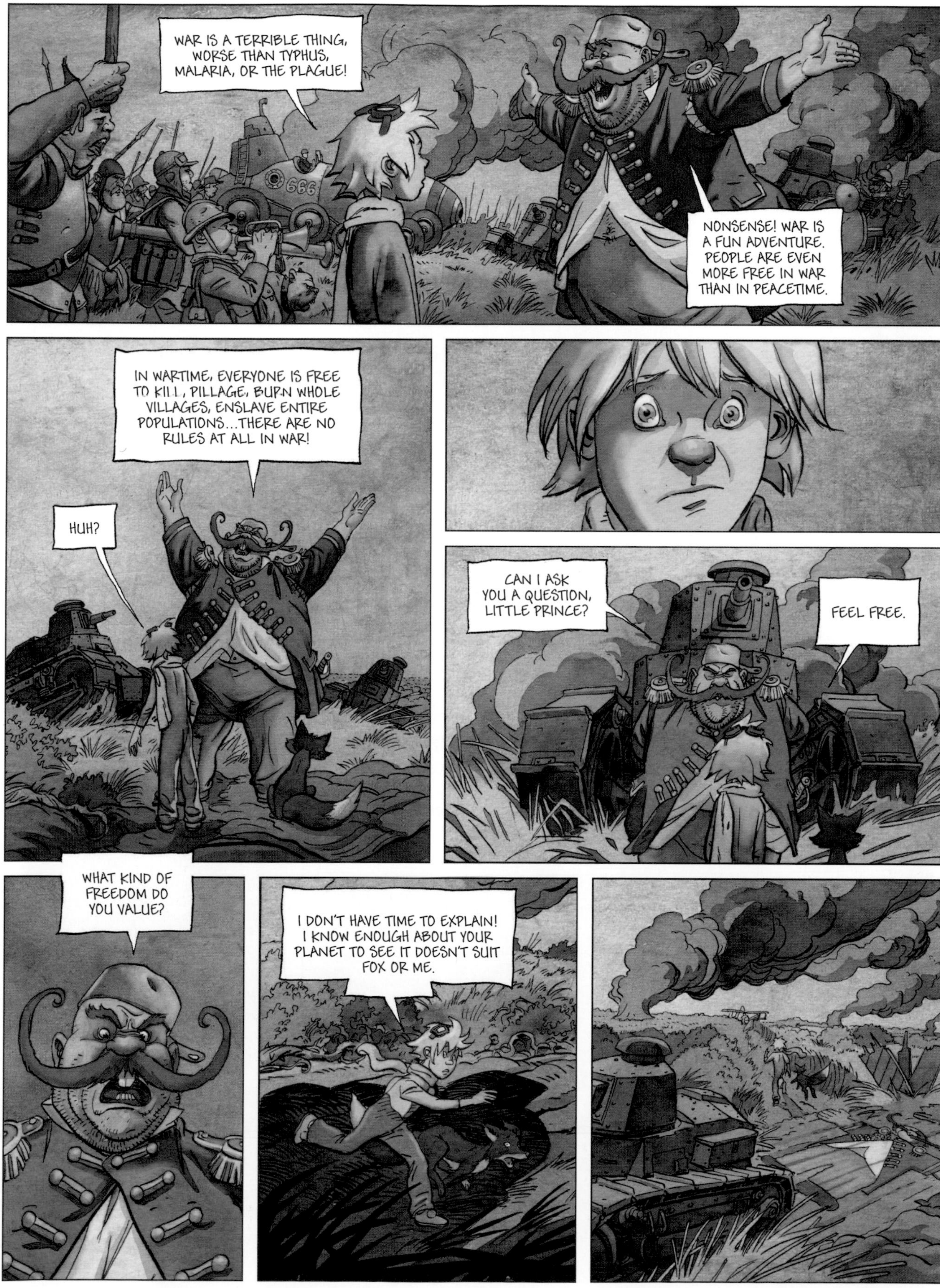
WAR IS A TERRIBLE THING, WORSE THAN TYPHUS, MALARIA, OR THE PLAGUE!
NONSENSE! WAR IS A FUN ADVENTURE. PEOPLE ARE EVEN MORE FREE IN WAR THAN IN PEACETIME.
IN WARTIME, EVERYONE IS FREE TO KILL, PILLAGE, BURN WHOLE VILLAGES, ENSLAVE ENTIRE POPULATIONS...THERE ARE NO RULES AT ALL IN WAR!
HUH?
CAN I ASK YOU A QUESTION, LITTLE PRINCE?
FEEL FREE.
WHAT KIND OF FREEDOM DO YOU VALUE?
I DON'T HAVE TIME TO EXPLAIN! I KNOW ENOUGH ABOUT YOUR PLANET TO SEE IT DOESN'T SUIT FOX OR ME.

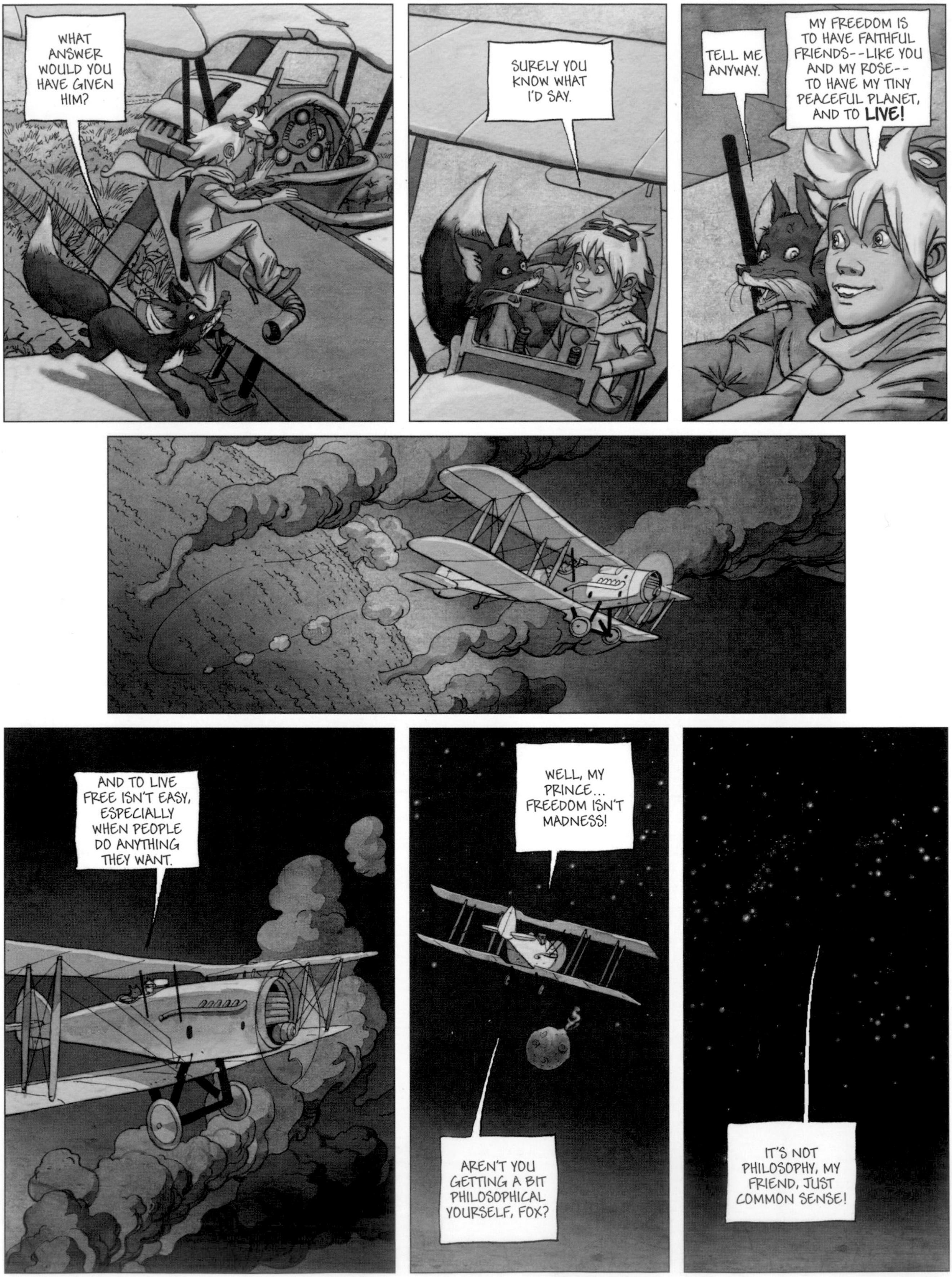
WHAT ANSWER WOULD YOU HAVE GIVEN HIM?
SURELY YOU KNOW WHAT I'D SAY.
TELL ME ANYWAY.
MY FREEDOM IS TO HAVE FAITHFUL FRIENDS--LIKE YOU AND MY ROSE-- TO HAVE MY TINY PEACEFUL PLANET, AND TO **LIVE!**
AND TO LIVE FREE ISN'T EASY, ESPECIALLY WHEN PEOPLE DO ANYTHING THEY WANT.
WELL, MY PRINCE... FREEDOM ISN'T MADNESS!
AREN'T YOU GETTING A BIT PHILOSOPHICAL YOURSELF, FOX?
IT'S NOT PHILOSOPHY, MY FRIEND, JUST COMMON SENSE!

ANTOINE DE SAINT-EXUPÉRY
Aviator • Author • Adventurer • Hero

Antoine de Saint-Exupéry, author of the novel *The Little Prince* on which these new adventures are based, was born on June 29, 1900, in Lyon, France. He was the third of five children: Marie-Madeleine, Simone, Antoine, François, and Gabrielle. It was when he was twelve years old, during his summer break from boarding school, that airplanes and flying first made a huge impression on him.

In 1920, he was accepted into the École des Beaux-Arts in Paris to study architecture, but the next year he joined the Second Aviation Regiment of the armed forces and received his pilot's license. In 1922, he had his first plane crash and suffered a head fracture. He had to leave the armed forces and work at different jobs on the ground to earn a living.

By May of 1926, Saint-Exupéry was able to fly again. He delivered airmail, which was a new and sometimes dangerous profession, on routes from France to Senegal and all the way to South America. That was where, in 1931, he met and married Consuelo Suncin.

From 1933 to 1938, Saint-Exupéry was very busy. He traveled to North Africa and Indochina and attempted to break the flight speed record from Paris to Saigon, Vietnam—during which his plane crashed again. It went down in the middle of the Sahara Desert. After his recovery, his life became even busier. He wrote newspaper reports in Spain on the Spanish Civil War, scouted airplane routes between Casablanca and Timbuktu, wrote a screenplay, registered several patents, and traveled to the United States. In 1939, with the start of World War II, he returned to France and talked his way into a job as a high-risk reconnaissance pilot for the French Air Force. But this only lasted until France reached an armistice agreement with Germany.

In December 1940, Saint-Exupéry returned to visit friends in New York, where he finally began work on *The Little Prince*. The story is narrated by a pilot who has crashed his plane into the Sahara Desert. He meets a little prince visiting from a faraway asteroid. Along the way, the prince also meets Fox and Snake. By late 1942, after spending the spring and summer writing and illustrating, Saint-Exupéry had completed his novel, and in April 1943 it was published in his native language of French *(Le Petit Prince)* and in English.

Saint-Exupéry was eager to return to the war. He decided to join the Free French Forces in Algeria, who were continuing the fight against the Axis powers. Because of his age, at first he had a hard time convincing them to let him fly. He was authorized to fly five dangerous missions. In fact, he flew eight. On July 31, 1944, Saint-Exupéry went on a scouting flight to prepare for military landings in the south of France. His plane disappeared over the water, and he was never seen again.

Over the decades since *The Little Prince* was published, it has gone on to become one of the best-selling novels of all time. In 2003, a small moon in our solar system's asteroid belt was named Petit-Prince in honor of the masterpiece Saint-Exupéry created.

The Little Prince in the Twenty-First Century

The Little Prince is a landmark of literature and one of the most translated and beloved books in the world. It tackles universal topics with a unique philosophical and poetic sensibility. Sixty-five years after the first edition, the Saint-Exupéry Estate decided to bring the character back for a whole new generation . . . and for everyone who has ever loved the boy who sees the world with his heart.

The Little Prince now returns in a series of new adventures that remain true to the spirit of the original work. He will travel from planet to planet chasing the wicked Snake, who wants to plunge the whole universe into darkness. On each planet, the Snake sends bad thoughts into the minds of its inhabitants, making them sad and grim, draining the life out of their planet. The Little Prince must leave his beautiful Rose behind and must use his vision and courage to defeat the Snake, bringing along his friend Fox to save planets in danger across the universe.

About the Adapters

After several years in video games and Japanese animation, adapter Guillaume Dorison became literary editor for the publisher Les Humanoïdes Associés in 2006, where he launched the Shogun Collection dedicated to original manga. In June 2010, he founded Élyum Studio with Didier Poli, Jean-Baptiste Hostache, and Xavier Dorison to provide services for the creation of graphic novels. In addition to his position as director of writing for Élyum Studio, he has more than two dozen comics and manga to his credit under the pseudonym IZU, has written several titles in the Explora series on world explorers for French publisher Glénat, and won the 2010 Animeland Prize for best French manga.

Didier Poli, artistic director for the new graphic novel adaptations based on *The Little Prince*, was born in Lyon in 1971. After graduate studies in applied arts, he worked for various animation studios including Disney. He was working as artistic director for the video game company Kalisto Entertainment when he met Manuel Bichebois in 2001 and began drawing Bichebois's graphic novel series L'Enfant de l'orage. At the 2004 Nîmes Festival, Didier Poli received the Bronze Boar prize for young talent. He continues, along with his work on graphic novels, to work regularly in cartoons and video games as a designer and storyboard artist.

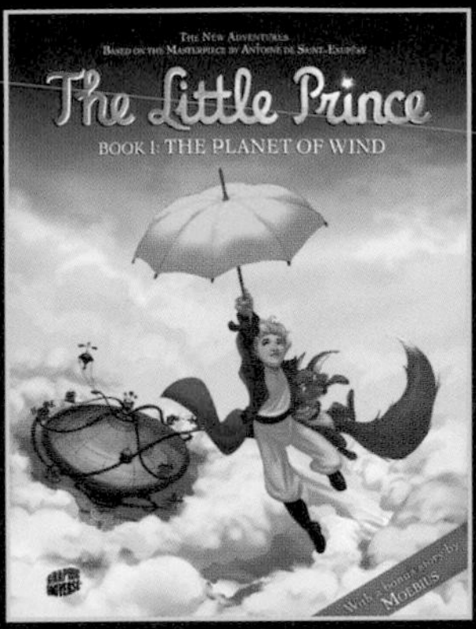
The New Adventures
Based on the Masterpiece by Antoine de Saint-Exupéry
The Little Prince
BOOK 1: THE PLANET OF WIND
MOEBIUS

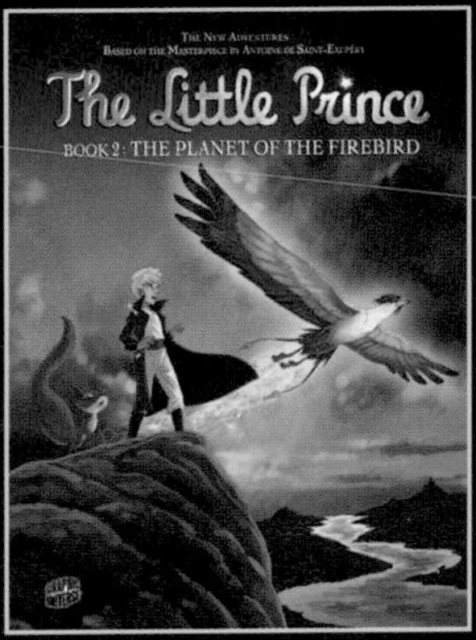
The New Adventures
Based on the Masterpiece by Antoine de Saint-Exupéry
The Little Prince
BOOK 2: THE PLANET OF THE FIREBIRD

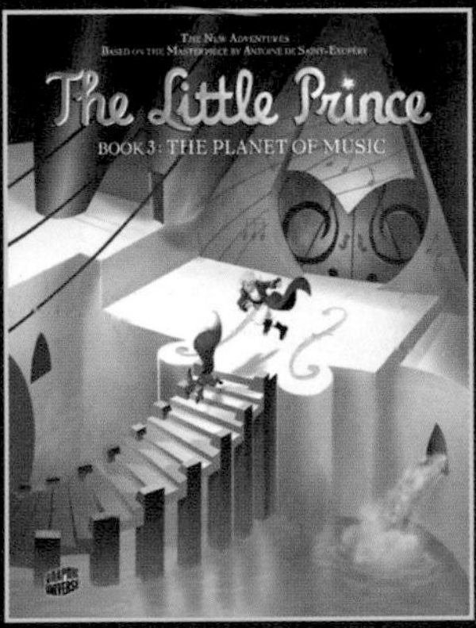
The New Adventures
Based on the Masterpiece by Antoine de Saint-Exupéry
The Little Prince
BOOK 3: THE PLANET OF MUSIC

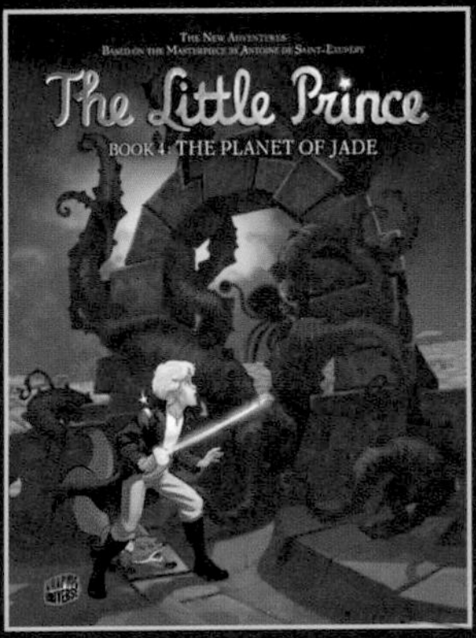
The New Adventures
Based on the Masterpiece by Antoine de Saint-Exupéry
The Little Prince
BOOK 4: THE PLANET OF JADE

Book 1: The Planet of Wind

Book 2: The Planet of the Firebird

Book 3: The Planet of Music

Book 4: The Planet of Jade

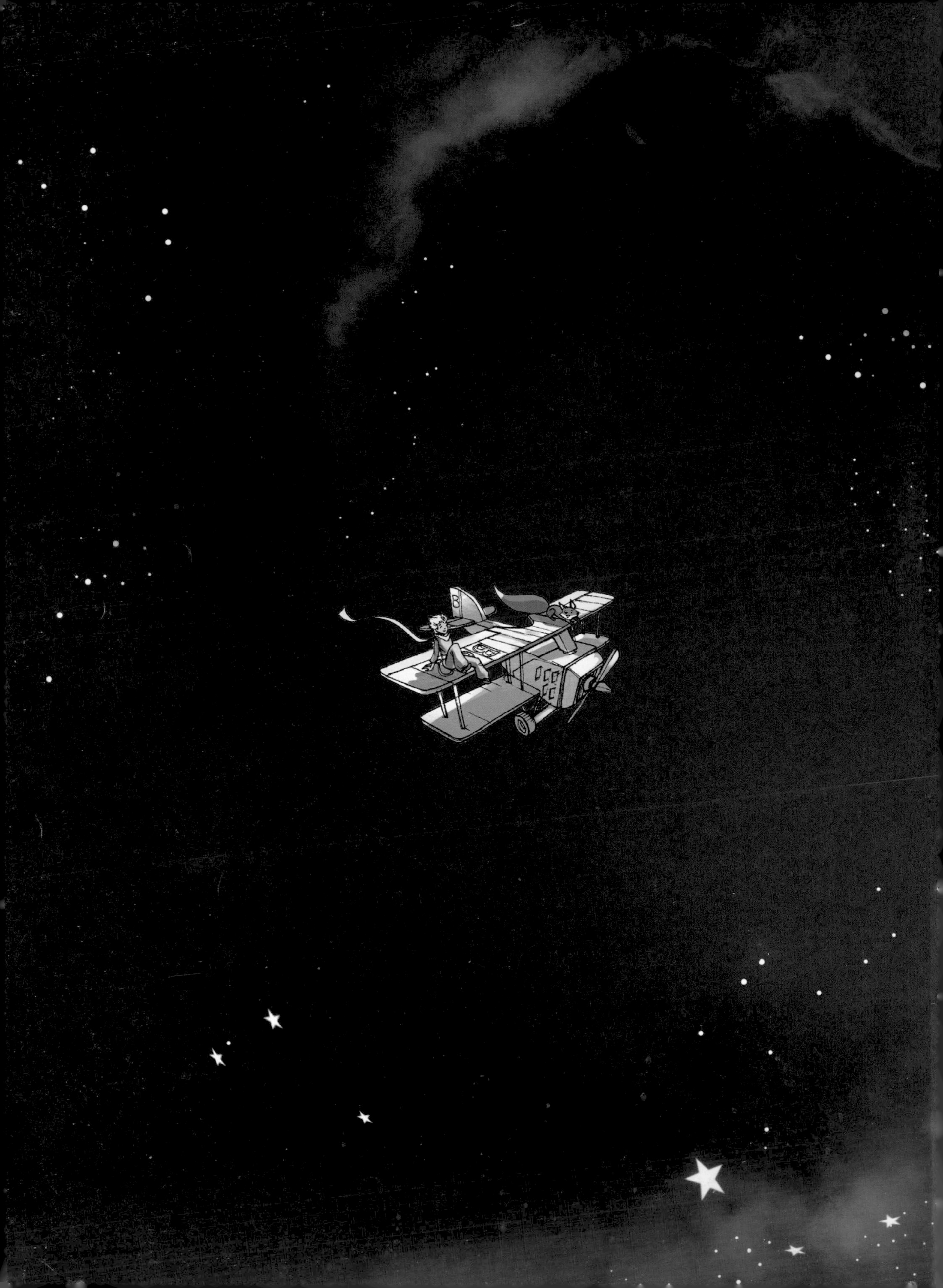
B